Skin

Also by
Adrienne Maria Vrettos

Sight

The Exile of Gigi Lane

Skin

Adrienne Maria Vrettos

MARGARET K. McELDERRY BOOKS
New York   London   Toronto   Sydney

MARGARET K. McELDERRY BOOKS

An imprint of Simon & Schuster Children's Publishing Division

1230 Avenue of the Americas, New York, New York 10020

This book is a work of fiction. Any references to historical events, real people, or real locales are used fictitiously. Other names, characters, places, and incidents are products of the author's imagination, and any resemblance to actual events or locales or persons, living or dead, is entirely coincidental.

Copyright © 2006 by Adrienne Maria Vrettos

All rights reserved, including the right of reproduction in whole or in part in any form.

MARGARET K. McELDERRY BOOKS is a trademark of Simon & Schuster, Inc.

For information about special discounts for bulk purchases, please contact Simon & Schuster Special Sales at 1-866-506-1949 or business@simonandschuster.com.

The Simon & Schuster Speakers Bureau can bring authors to your live event.

For more information or to book an event, contact the Simon & Schuster Speakers Bureau at 1-866-248-3049 or visit our website at www.simonspeakers.com.

Also available in a hardcover edition.

Book design by Yaffa Jaskoll

The text for this book is set in Manticore.

Manufactured in the United States of America

First paperback edition October 2007

4 6 8 10 9 7 5 3

The Library of Congress has cataloged the hardcover edition as follows:

Library of Congress Cataloging-in-Publication Data

Vrettos, Adrienne Maria.

Skin / Adrienne Maria Vrettos.—1st ed.

p. cm.

Summary: When his parents decide to separate, eighth-grader Donnie watches with horror as the physical condition of his sixteen-year-old sister, Karen, deteriorates due to an eating disorder.

ISBN 978-1-4169-0655-1 (hc)

[1. Brothers and sisters—Fiction. 2. Anorexia nervosa—Fiction. 3. Family problems—Fiction. 4. Self-perception—Fiction.] I. Title.

PZ7.V9855Sk 2006

[Fic]—dc22

2005001119

ISBN 978-1-4169-0656-8 (pbk)

For Miriam Cohen, who believed

These are the things you think when you come home to find that your sister has starved herself to death and you have dropped to your knees to revive her:

1. My sister is flat like a board. There's fat guys in the locker room with bigger boobs than she has.
2. When I scream my sister's name into her face, I can hear my father's voice in my own.
3. Where is it you're supposed to press? In the middle, on the side? Left or right?

I choose middle. I put the heels of my hands, one on top of the other, on Karen's chest. I can feel her ribs under the thick of her too-small sweater. When I press down, her head rocks a little, hanging huge on her neck. I feel nothing pulse against my hand. I count out, "One and two and three and four and five." Something cracks under my palm and I yank my hands away, not because I broke her rib but because she did nothing. I broke her and she didn't even flinch.

"COME ON!" I scream. I shove my fingers into her mouth and pull it open. Her teeth move against my fingers. I suck in a breath and push it out, into her. Her chest rises. Fake alive. She doesn't return my breath.

"Karen?" I whisper.

The front door crashes open and whacks me in the shoulder, knocking me away. I land on my side, my elbow smacking against the tile of the front-hall floor. When I look up at the doorway, I see God. I sit up, the arm with the bruised elbow limp and tingling in my lap. God is huge; he stands in the doorway and blocks the winter sun from slanting into the hall. He's holding a box of fishing tackle. It takes me a second to realize it's not God. But it is Elvis. Elvis is back. He is an EMT with a harelip and acne, and he has come to save my sister.

I am in the center of his shadow, and when he steps into the house to drop his equipment at Karen's side, the brightness of the sun surprises me, burning red-ringed white spots into my eyes before I can turn my face to where Elvis is pressing two fingers behind Karen's jaw.

I crawl toward him, my hurt arm curled against my

stomach. I watch his face, trying to read what he feels beneath his fingers. I am whispering, "Please please please please please."

He moves his hand away from her neck and I choke on the air in my mouth.

"How old is she?" he asks, and I know it's a question meant to keep me from being strangled by my own throat, it is supposed to get air into my lungs and back out again.

"Sixteen." The word squeaks out and I am gulping air and I am saying too loudly, "She is sixteen and I am fourteen. I'm her brother."

"Turn on the light," Elvis says, still not looking at me.

I scramble up and switch on the front-hall light and press my back against the wall. Elvis sucks in his breath when the light hits my sister. I could gouge out his eyes for that. For looking at her and gasping. For making maybe the last thing she hears be some jerkoff gasping at the skin hanging loose off her bones.

I've seen dead things before. I know a dead thing looks smaller than when it was alive. My sister looks like she could fold inside a paper cup.

There is another EMT in the house now and she kneels next to Elvis so he can talk low into her ear. Behind them, in the kitchen, I can see the calendar that hangs by the phone. There is an empty square where today's date should be. I know what was in that blank space, I know it was more than a number to show that today is February twenty-second. Months and months ago Karen and Amanda decorated that small square because today is the one-year anniversary of the day they met and became instant best friends. They had a whole celebration planned. Karen said, "Donnie, you have to play yourself in the historical reenactment of the first time I met Amanda."

It's not till Elvis says, "Let us work, son," that I realize I am walking toward the kitchen, toward the memory of Karen and Amanda bending their heads over the calendar on the kitchen table. I've stepped onto the bright orange backboard the other EMT brought in with her. She lays her hand on my shin and pushes gently. I lean back up against the wall. "Let us work," she says.

"Let us work" means "let us put our hands on her." Let us open her eyes and let them slip shut again. Let us shine lights into her mouth and put our palms on her chest and press again and again and again until Elvis sits back on his heels and shakes his head and says, "Son of a bitch."

I'm telling you this because you didn't ask. I've got it all here, growing like a tumor in my throat. I'm telling you because if I don't, I will choke on it. Everybody knows what happened, but nobody asks. And Elvis the EMT doesn't count because when he asked, he didn't even listen to me answer because he was listening to my sister's heart not beat with his stethoscope. I want to tell. It's mine to tell. Even if you didn't ask, you have to hear it.

A car door slams, and when I look outside, I see Mom

come screaming up the front steps gripping her brown leather purse by the top of its strap like a weapon swinging from her fisted hand. Karen's on a gurney now and Elvis is pulling the sheet over her face when Mom runs past me and launches screaming into the air. I look away when she is midflight, flinging herself over Karen, collapsing the gurney with her weight. Mom's left index finger gets smashed in the workings of the gurney, and later Elvis puts it in a splint while Mom lies on the couch, her eyes open and not blinking.

I am still standing by the light switch, and I am trying to remember when it was that Karen painted over that small square on the calendar.

1

Karen almost jerks my shoulder out of its socket dragging me
out of the house and onto the front stoop. We stand huffing
on the top step in the February air for a second. I nod at her,
impressed. She nods back and bends over, hands on her
knees. We're like athletes. Sprint runners. Sprint runners spe-
cially trained to run into burning houses to rescue orphans.
Except we don't run into houses, we run out of them. And our
house isn't burning, at least not with fire. We're out here
because Karen freaks out when Mom and Dad fight. She
always has. As soon as one of them so much as cocks an eye-
brow, Karen is out the door. She grabs me by the wrist and
drags me out after her. She's done it since we were kids.

She says she used to keep an old and smelly lunch box by
the door, filled with a spare diaper, a bottle, a box of crackers,

and these earmuffs that were shaped like teddy bears. She'd make me wear the earmuffs, even in summer, because I was always either getting or getting over an ear infection. She thought the teddy bears helped. Over the years we lost the earmuffs, but I kept the ear infections. We have much better provisions now. I reach over the side of the steps and slide out the loose brick. I pull out the tin box, replace the brick, and sit on the top step. Karen sits next to me and hands me my science book. She'd be the best and worst person to have with you if your house actually were on fire. She'd tear you out of the house before you got a whiff of smoke, but the only thing she'd rescue besides you is your homework.

She opens her Spanish workbook, and I open the tin.

"What do you want?" I ask.

"Do we have any caramel chews left? Zip up your jacket."

"No caramel. There's peanut, though," I say, zipping my jacket to my chin and burying the bottom half of my face in its high neck.

"Fine," she says, reaching over and yanking my hood up over my head. She zips her own jacket and takes a handful of the peanut candies from me. I go to work on a half-eaten box of Valentine's Day chocolates left over from last week. I can tell Karen's listening to Mom and Dad, pretending to be reading. She would never bring us farther than the front steps. We go far enough so that we don't have to see it up close, but we're close enough so nothing really bad can happen. They know we're out here.

It's already almost too dark to read my science book. I open it anyway and let my eyes unfocus on the page until the ink and the paper blend together. Then I slam the book shut and look at Karen. Her nose has turned bright red from the cold.

"I'll make you macaroni later," she says, not looking up from the book that I know she can't see. She used to tell me this to calm me down, to keep me from banging my fists and my knees against the front door, trying to get back in. She always made good on her promise. When they were done fighting, when Dad had sulked off and Mom had locked herself in the bathroom, we'd slink inside. Karen would make macaroni and we'd pretend it was just us living there.

I rest my chin on the edge of my book and start thinking about how if I were in the woods, way up on a mountain, instead of on my front steps, this time of night would be really scary.

Especially if something went terribly wrong with the mission that me and the rest of my highly trained team of secret service assassins were on. We made camp for the night in a small clearing, surrounded by towering pine trees that swayed and creaked in the cold wind. I am on first watch with Harley, the most loveable screw-up I've ever served with. Midway into our shift, I elbow him in the gut to wake him up and tell him I'm going to take a leak. I step outside of the circle of firelight and go to the edge of the woods. Midstream, the reflection of the fire suddenly disappears from the leaves I'm peeing on. I finish fast and turn around to whisper-yell, "H! You asshole. What'd you do? Piss on the fire? Harley? Stop dicking around and bring some wood." I curse under my breath while I relight the fire. What I see as the fire slowly lights the camp makes me drop to the ground and pull out my gun. They're gone. My whole team, all of them. Harley. Everybody. The tents have been slashed, the sleeping bags are empty, and there are drops of blood on the ground leading out of our campsite and into the woods. I remember Captain's words during training. He called me the wild card, a loose cannon. If it were up to him, I'd be guarding some eighth-term-senator's grandmother, not the president's daughter. But it's not up to him. Me and the president go way back, further back than I'd ever be able to tell a soul without turning up dead somewhere. The president wanted me on this, and now that his daughter has been kidnapped, it is up to me to save her. Captain would want me to do the safe thing: wait till morning. I can hear his raspy voice, *There's no telling what's in these woods, soldier.* "Only one way to find out," I say aloud. I grab my night-vision goggles and my pack, and head into the darkness.

"Who's that?"

Up, up out of the woods and back to where my butt has frozen to our top step, Karen's actually looked up from her book to watch a crooked rust-red pickup truck that's parking at the house across the street.

"Must be the new people," I say. Mom said someone had

moved in. I just assumed it was another old couple, like the one who lived there before. The two of them had looked like brother and sister; twins even, except they were married. Creepy.

A really big guy in a parka you'd wear if you were climbing polar ice caps is getting out of the driver's side of the truck. He looks like one of those guys that builds houses. Or tears them down. Either way, he'd do it with his bare hands. He stretches when he's out, and sees us watching from across the street. He waves.

"Hiya." His voice rolls like rocks across the street. The passenger-side door opens, and a soccer ball falls out and rolls under the truck. The big man picks it up. Karen and I are both watching to see who gets out. I'm hoping for a kid my age, someone I could hang out with all weekend, till school on Monday when he finds out I'm a leper and pretends not to know me. The truck door opens farther and someone gets out. It's not a kid my age. But it is the most beautiful girl I've ever seen. Roll your eyes if you want. You think of a better way to say it when you see someone and every single part of you stops for a second, and then starts up again, but in a way that will never be the same.

Karen's already standing. She pulls me up by my jacket sleeve.

"Hi. I'm Karen," she calls as I stare at the girl crossing the street toward us. Her hair's pulled back in a ponytail and she's wearing a soccer uniform under her jacket. She's been sweating.

"This is Donnie," Karen says, nudging me with her elbow. "Did you just move in?"

"Yep. I'm Amanda. You live here?" Her socks are doubled down, showing her shin guards. She's got a scab the size of a dime on her right knee. The skin around the scab is lighter than the rest of her.

"Yep," I say. I can't look her in the eye. So I look at her chest until Karen elbows me in the ribs.

"Yeah, we live here," Karen says, as if my answer wasn't good enough. I hate it when she does that.

"So . . . what are you guys doing out here? Aren't you cold?" Amanda asks, resting the toe of her cleat on the edge of the step. I stare at the lines of her leg muscle and wonder how Karen will answer this one. From inside we all hear Mom yell, "The hell I don't!"

"Family tradition," Karen says quickly. Good answer. Amanda nods and smiles.

"What grade are you in?" Karen and Amanda ask each other the question at the same time and laugh.

"I'm in tenth," Karen says.

"Me too," Amanda says. "I start at Kennedy on Monday. I just met with the coach for the indoor league."

Karen nods toward me. "He's in—"

"I'm in eighth," I interrupt, and Karen snorts. Amanda smiles at me and I try to tuck my entire head inside my jacket.

"Dad and I just got Chinese food if you want to come over. It'll be warmer inside than out here."

"Sure!" I say. That's a lie: I don't *say* it, I practically scream it from inside my jacket.

Amanda and Karen both look at me.

"Sure," Karen says. "Thanks."

I don't notice that it's gone quiet inside till Mom opens the front door and comes out wearing her stupid fake smile and talking in her stupid fake voice.

"Hi there! I'm Karen's mom."

Apparently Karen's an only child.

"You must have just moved in across the street."

"Yes ma'am. My dad and I did."

"Well, tell your dad we would love to have the two of you over for dinner sometime real soon."

"Okay. Thanks."

Mom's eyes are red-rimmed and glassy. Through the door I can see Dad pacing. He's not done yet. We all stand there for a second, looking at our feet.

Amanda says, "I actually just asked if . . . they wanted to eat at our house tonight. We're having Chinese. There's plenty."

I hold in my mouth the taste of Amanda including me, and watch Mom.

"Well, sure, Karen can eat at your house. Donnie, you don't want to hang around girls all night, do you? You'll stay here with us."

I look back inside the house. Dad's standing still now, watching us from the living room. I look back at Karen, trying to grab onto her with my eyes. I think *Don't leave me, don't leave me, don't leave me.* She leaves me.

"Okay. Bye, Mom. I'll be home later."

"Nice meeting you, Donnie," Amanda says.

I watch them walk down the driveway; their heads already tipped toward each other, Amanda linking elbows with Karen as if they've been best friends forever. I'm left to follow Mom into the house as she is answering Dad's demand, "Who was that?"

I don't blame Karen. I would have left too, if I could have.

2

I have goose bumps from the air conditioning. Dad's managed to make it feel like winter in the car, instead of the first day of our summer vacation. Mom keeps staring at the console and then fluttering her hand up, like she's going to change it.

"It's fine, Diane."

Even with the air on there is a sheen of sweat on Dad's forehead. Mom is sitting with her arms folded in her lap, moving them occasionally to rub her upper arms. I can see she has goose bumps too. She shakes her head and looks out the window.

It started this morning, with Mom walking through the house a second time to make sure everything was closed up and turned off and unplugged. Dad and Karen and I were already waiting by the car, loading in our magazines and music and the car-game books that we'd found in the attic. With the car loaded I stood on the back bumper, balancing my weight on first one foot and then the other. Karen leaned against the hood with Dad.

"What's she doing?" Dad looks at his watch and then scowls toward the hills. The highway's on the other side. I can see him calculate how many more cars are going to be on the road for every second Mom makes us wait.

"Probably calling Aunt Janice again," Karen mumbles. Dad doesn't answer. He's still mad. Aunt Janice, Uncle Dan, and my cousin Bobby were supposed to have shared the lake house with us this summer, but Uncle Dan had to get an emergency hernia operation so now they can't come. Mom cried when she found out. I could hear her whispering on her bedroom phone, saying, "I need you there, Jannie." Dad's just mad because it was too late to get a smaller lake house, so now we have to "pay for way more house than we need." Cousin Bobby and I were supposed to have shared a room. For the past few months I'd been trying to imagine what it'd be like, but I could never get a clear picture in my head. Whenever Bobby visits, I have the urge to wrap myself around his leg like I did when I was a little kid. Back then I did it because it was fun to sit on his foot while he dragged me around the house, but now it'd be to get him to stand still, to stay longer, to stay forever. I still pretend we're brothers, and that next time he comes he'll stay for good. He'll go to my school and be my best friend, and everyone will see how cool he is and then they'll know, if he's friends with me, then I'm not the loser they think I am. When we found out that none of them were coming, Karen snorted and said, "Sucks for you, Donnie," and then in the same breath, "Can Amanda come up then? We have room now."

"I don't know what Mom's doing," Karen answers.

I lose my balance and step heavily onto the driveway.

"Donnie, go get Mom."

"You go get her!" I step back up onto the bumper, back up onto the narrow rod of metal that I have to cross to reach the little kid that's trapped in the burning school. I'll have to walk across, like a tightrope walker. This is for the tightrope championship. If I can walk across this line, over the pit of snarling tigers, I will be declared the best tightrope walker ever.

"Honey? You about ready?" Dad calls, still leaning against the car, trusting his voice will make it through the open front door. Mom finally comes out with a jolly face and tired eyes.

"Just checking everything!"

Mom opens up the passenger-side door and then looks over the roof of the car at Dad, who's giving one last yank on the cord holding our possessions to the roof rack.

"Did you unplug the TV?" Mom's biggest fear is that one of our appliances will burst into flames while we're on vacation.

Dad doesn't answer. He just stares at her, blank faced and blinking.

"I'm just going to go double-check," Mom says, already rushing back toward the house.

I'm about to take my last step, the step that will make me tightrope champion, but decide it will be more exciting to fall into the pit of tigers and have to fight them off with my kung fu skills. I jump onto the driveway and kick my leg up high, almost as high as the roof of the car. Karen watches and rolls her eyes, so I kick again, this time close to her face. I forget how quick she is when she wants to be and she grabs my foot mid-kick and holds it up, laughing her head off while I hop around and shout, "You think you have me, evil sister? Just wait till I demolish you with my signature black falcon flying kick!"

But I can't really kick, so I pull a hair out of her arm instead, which on the good side makes her drop my foot, but on the bad side, she's put me in a headlock before I can finish telling her that I just got her with my unbeatable yanking-hair torture. I'm really happy Dad's too busy glowering at the house to yell at us to stop. But after a second he makes us get in the car, and once we get in, he turns the key in the ignition. I look at Karen, wondering if we're just going to go on vacation without Mom, leaving her to check and recheck that she unplugged the iron and the toaster and the microwave. Karen shrugs and puts on her headphones, which means *Don't talk to me, I'm busy looking moody.*

"Dad, can we go fishing up there?" I lean forward so my body is wedged between the two front seats.

"If we ever get there, yes we can go fishing," he answers.

I ignore his tone.

"Cool," I say. "We can catch dinner."

Dad smirks and nods his head. I have an urge to ask, "Hey, Dad, why do you have to be such an asshole all the time?" I actually get as far as "Hey, Dad," but Mom gets in the car before I have the chance to see if I have the guts to say the whole thing.

Dad's hands are tight on the steering wheel and he won't look at Mom. He just twists around so he can back the car out of the driveway.

"Ready?" Mom asks as she turns in her seat to grin at us. We smile at her, both of us. But it's the look you give someone you feel sorry for, a smile that barely makes your mouth move and doesn't affect the rest of your face. Mom turns around and leans forward to adjust the temperature. Dad glares at her, and turns the knob back to where it was. She looks at him, and then pulls her book from her bag and starts reading. That's how it got so damn cold in the car.

After an hour Karen pulls off her headphones and says, "Dad, Donnie's turning blue."

Dad glances at me in the rearview mirror. I'm not turning blue, but he turns down the air anyway and looks at Mom. He winks at her and she wrinkles her nose at him.

Karen rolls her eyes and takes out a deck of cards. We all understand what just happened. They made up. Now we can stop ignoring each other.

"Donnie, let's have a good summer," Karen says, loud.

"Yeah," I say. Just as loud.

Mom and Dad ignore us.

"So . . . when's Amanda coming up?" I try to say it like I don't really care, like I'm just making conversation to pass the time.

"Next week. After soccer camp."

"Hmm," I say.

"Chris and Bean aren't coming?" Karen asks.

I answer quickly, "They're at camp all summer."

Karen raises her eyebrows. I ignore her and look at my cards. I know she is trying to solve the same riddle that's in my head. The riddle is this: What happened between me and my two best friends to make them scrape me out of their lives like dog crap off a sneaker? I think about last summer, trying again to find some sign of what was to come.

"This is for the championship."

I give the ceremonial bow to Chris and Bean, who sit on deck chairs sharing the last crumbs of a bag of chips. Bean is wrapped in three towels and an afghan that Chris's mom keeps out here for him. Bean's what they call a "fragile" kid. That's why he and Chris make the perfect odd-couple combination. Bean's about the size of a mini Tootsie Roll and Chris is the only kid going into the eighth grade who buys clothes at the Big and Tall store at the mall. They're best friends with each other, and I'm best friends with the two of them at the same time. Not individually, though, because they already have each other.

I step onto the diving board, my eye on the sun as it bleeds red orange into the horizon. I wait till only a sliver of the burning disk can be seen above the hills. I want to hit the water right when the sun on the last day of the best summer I've ever had slips behind the round edge of the world. I hold my arms over my head and curl my toes over the edge of the diving board. I bounce once, readying myself mind and body to steal the cannonball championship trophy (aka a giant stick of beef jerky Chris's dad sent him from Texas) from its proud perch on Chris's desk.

I give a silent count, *Three, two, . . .*

"ALL EYES ARE ON DONALD LEPLANT!" Chris's shout almost makes me fall off the board; I windmill my arms till I get my balance.

"Knock it off!" I shout, laughing, at Chris. Bean tries to stuff one of his towels into Chris's mouth, yelling to me, "Do it, Donnie! You've worked all summer for this! Do it!" and then "Get off me!" as Chris sits on him. I count down again. Out of the corner of my eye I can see Bean squirm free and take off into the backyard. I jump, curling tightly into a ball, tensing my back for the slap of the water. As I go in, I see Chris and Bean look up from where they're wrestling on the grass. It's a big splash, I can feel it. I push off against the bottom of the pool and come up to hear Bean clapping and hollering and Chris rolling on the ground, shouting, "I demand a rematch!" I pump a victory fist in the air and go back under, pushing myself down till I hover just above the pool bottom.

I don't want this summer to end. I want to keep coming over here every day. I want to keep eating peanut butter and jelly sandwiches and chips on the deck every day for lunch. I want Chris to keep imitating his mom after she yells at us for splashing water out of the pool. I want the summer to stretch out in front of me forever. I hold my breath till it gushes out of me, and I rise to the surface.

"I'm glad they're not coming. Those guys are pricks," Karen says.

I'm so deep in the memory I almost say, "No, they're not," but I stop myself, because I know she's right. They turned on me. I wish they'd just sat me down at the beginning of the school year and said, "You're out," instead of deciding together to drop me and waiting to see when I'd notice. If they'd done that, sat me down and told me, I would have laughed in their faces. I would have gotten up and walked away and left them sitting there to realize what they'd just done. It's not like there's a whole line of kids waiting to be friends with us, clamoring to take my place. We're the end of the line. We're the ones that people look at and think, *At least I'm not them.* Kids get a death grip on their friends when it looks like they might be slipping down to where we are. It's like a kick in the balls, when people use you as a threat, when you hear someone say, "Stop being such a douche bag or we'll make you go sit with LePlant and the other freaks." If someone asked why it was us, why we were the bottom of the barrel, I'd say, "Open your eyes, dumbass." Nothing about us is right. We're the wrongest kids you've ever seen. Our faces are wrong with zits, we have the wrong hair, the wrong clothes, and I think that we might be ugly. Our families are wrong because none of us are rich, our bodies are wrong because we suck at sports, and there's something really wrong with all of our personalities, because nobody likes us, not even the teachers. Teachers make fun of us too, and think we don't notice.

It's other things too. It's the time everyone saw Bean crying on the phone to his mom in the office, or when Chris split his pants from back to front bending over to pick up a dropped chocolate bar, or the month I had to have cotton stuffed in my ears every day because yellow puss was leaking out of them and whenever I was around, everyone was doing these really exaggerated imitations of what they thought deaf kids sound like when they talk. They basically made grunting sounds and found different ways to flip me off using their own brand of sign language, even though I kept saying that I could hear fine. They would yell it back at me, in their fake deaf voices. I finally just ignored them, pretended I was deaf, and when I got better and the cotton came out, they went back to ignoring me. Bean washes his hands before and after every class and turns door handles with an elbow or a foot instead of touching them with his hands. Every once in a while he'll run screaming down the hallway while someone chases him with a pencil they say they stuck in a full toilet. Chris keeps pitching tents in his sweatpants during gym. And there's other reasons that I don't even know how to name, because for the life of me I can't tell what they are. Something has to be really wrong with us that we can't see, for us to be where we are in the school cool chain. Because for everything that's "wrong" with us, there's some other kid with the exact same affliction who somehow still manages to have a good life.

For whatever reason, Chris and Bean decided that for all the things wrong with them, whatever was wrong with me was even worse. They started to act like I was bothering them, tagging along like a little brother. I already knew what that felt like. They'd be talking in the hall and I'd walk up to them and Chris would say something like, "Donnie, why do you have to follow us around? Go get us a table for lunch." So I should have just dumped them, right? Stopped hanging out with them. Found other friends. But there were no other friends. No one moved up from where we were. You stayed there till you dropped out or transferred or graduated and didn't get invited to any graduation parties. So I'd go save us a stupid table for lunch and maybe they'd come, and maybe they wouldn't. But they never cut me off altogether. They always left me a little hope that things would be the way they were, to make sure I stayed around. I guess I do know what happened. They just realized that crapping on someone could make them feel better about being crapped on themselves.

I was spending more and more time out on the front steps while Mom and Dad fought. If Karen was home, she'd take me over to Amanda's with her, but most times she didn't even come home after school. She just went straight to

Amanda's. I'd see how long it took her to look out Amanda's bedroom window and notice me sitting in front of our house. She'd come over, stomp past me up the steps, and practically kick open our front door. She'd never go inside. She'd just lean in and yell something like, "Mom! It's six thirty and Donnie needs his dinner!"

I'd mumble, "I'm not a three-year-old, you know."

Mom and Dad would shut up for a second, and then Mom would yell back something along the lines of, "Why are you telling *me*? Am I the only one in this family who knows where the kitchen is? Everyone in this house turns into the village idiot whenever there's actual work to be done! 'Uh, what do you mean, cook something? A vacuum? What's that?'" This is directed at Dad.

Karen waits and listens till she hears Dad mumble something and Mom yells, "*You* worked all day? Housework *is* work! Donnie! Come inside. It's cold out."

On her way back down the steps Karen would say, "Tell her I'm eating at Amanda's."

Every time, I'd kind of hope that Karen wouldn't come over. I wanted her to let me take care of Mom and Dad in my own way. I wish she'd let me sit out there till Mom and Dad finally noticed and had to chip away the ice that'd formed on me while I waited.

3

"It's up ahead, Joseph."

Karen and I are both asleep in the backseat, and I wake up thinking we're at the lake house. We're not. We're slowing down on a two-lane road. On the side of the road a line of cars are parked and people are standing around with binoculars looking into a swamp.

"I used to come here with Dad," Mom says. She looks at Dad, and I see him deciding between ignoring her and smiling. Next to me I can feel Karen relax when the sides of his mouth finally curl up.

"The road was just one lane then," she says. "It wasn't even paved. We would come here with ham sandwiches and chips in a paper-bag lunch and look at the birds."

Mom's the best when she unclenches.

Dad lays his hand on Mom's thigh and says, "Kids, you know what else happened out here?"

Mom laughs and looks at Dad, leaning her head back against the seat, waiting for Dad to tell us.

"I proposed to your mom out here."

"No shit!" Karen laughs. "Really?"

"Yes, Pottymouth, really. I took your dad out here the first weekend he came home with me from college to meet my dad and your Aunt Janice."

"I waited till your mom was in the shower, and then I asked her dad's permission."

"What'd he say?" I ask. I know the answer's obvious, but it's so rare that Dad tells any sort of story, you kind of have to help him along.

"Well, first he looked at me and grunted, and then said, 'You hurt her and I'll pickle your liver.' Bet you never knew that, did you?" he says to Mom, raising his eyebrows.

She looks at him a second, biting her lip, and then starts to laugh so hard she's not making any noise, she's not even breathing.

Karen and I look at each other, and Dad looks at Mom. She's got tears running down her face. Finally she gasps out, "I did know! Janice was hiding on the stairs when Daddy said that! She scared me to death! She ran into the bathroom and tore the shower curtain straight off its rod trying to get it open, and she was trying to whisper but she was laughing and crying so hard she just kept hiccuping. She finally jumped in the shower with me, fully clothed, and sputtered out that you were going to ask me to marry you. So I screamed and laughed and cried, and she cried and laughed, and then we just hugged each other and cried till we were laughing again."

Mom's crying now—laughing, but crying. She wipes her face and beams at Dad. "I hadn't thought about that in a long time."

Dad's quiet.

Karen is leaning forward in the seat, her chin on Mom's shoulder.

"Mom, why were you crying?"

Mom kisses Karen on the cheek.

"Partly because I was happy. But partly because everything was about to change. It wouldn't be me and Janice anymore."

"Hmm," Karen says, sitting back in her seat.

"Donnie," Dad says, looking at me in the mirror, "maybe one day you'll be lucky enough to have the woman you love cry when she finds out that you want to marry her."

What the fuck do I say to that? He's not even saying it to me. He's saying it to Mom, who just sighs and snaps, "Oh, you know that's not what I meant."

Dad shrugs and turns up the radio. Mom looks out the window, occasionally laughing out loud again and then saying, "I'm sorry, I'm sorry. I'll stop."

There's a road stand a few miles past the swamp.

"You kids want to stop?" Dad asks.

"I'm not hungry," Karen says immediately.

"Come on, Karen." Mom turns around and winks at her. "It's vacation. Calories don't count when you're on vacation."

"I'm hungry," I say.

"You can pull over, but I'm not eating anything." Karen's leaning forward, talking right into Dad's ear.

Dad pulls into a space in the parking lot and we all get out of the car, reaching up and out to stretch our back and arms. Mom bends over till her fingers are brushing the pavement. Karen is staring at Mom's butt, her lips curled.

"God, Mom, do you have to do that?"

Mom is still bending over. "Oh, I'm sorry, Karen, is my behind embarrassing you?" She starts to shake her rear, and Karen gets back in the car and slams the door and refuses to look out the window.

"You guys are no fun," Mom says, standing up straight and hurrying to catch up with Dad and me who are already walking toward the end of the line that starts at the window where people are ordering. Mom links her arm through Dad's and says, "Come on, it's vacation. It's supposed to be fun." Dad nods, his eyes still on the menu.

"What are you going to get Karen?" he asks.

Mom sighs. "Well, she has to eat something." She studies the menu.

There's a girl in front of us in line. Really short blond hair. I think we must be close to the lake because she's wearing the top of a bikini and shorts. She has a tiny mole right above where the bikini ties under her hair. Her shorts are low, and if I lean forward the tiniest bit I can see the top rim of her bikini bottom and the pale strip of skin where her tan line stops. What if she's our neighbor at the lake? What if one night their electricity goes out and her family has to come stay with us? What if Mom and Dad and Karen aren't home and it's just me? What if their house doesn't lose electricity, but the rest of her family does get lost hiking and she comes to our house and she asks if she can sleep over because she's scared? What if she doesn't want to sleep in a room alone and asks if she can sleep with—

"Donnie." Dad brings me out of my stupor. "What would you like? They have hamburgers, hot dogs, French fries . . ."

"I can read, Dad," I say, but then quickly add, "I'll have a cheeseburger and fries," so he knows I'm not mad at him. That's a lie. I am mad at him. I'm mad because he's being a jerk to Mom. But he's my dad, and we're on vacation, and everyone is already fighting, and I don't want to add to it, so I ask, "What are you getting?" just to keep the conversation going.

We get our food and Dad doesn't want to lose any driving time, so we're going to eat on the road. When we get back to the car with our food, Karen has her feet hanging out the rolled-down window, bouncing to whatever is playing on her headphones. A kid with a shaved head and a neck tattoo is across the parking lot staring at Karen, and she's staring back in that challenging way she has that doesn't let you look away. I block her view.

"Move over," I say. "You're in my seat."

While Karen scoots over, I turn and try to give the shaved-head kid a death look, a don't-mess-with-my-sister look. But now he's too busy making out with the blond short-haircut girl to notice. His left hand is low on her back, the tips of his fingers hidden in her waistband. Figures.

I get in the car just in time for the battle. Mom is turned around in her seat, holding a packet of French fries out to my sister, who says loudly, over the music on her headphones, "Mom, I told you, I'm not hungry."

"Turn down the music. You haven't eaten since we left the house."

"I had grapes," Karen says, ignoring what Mom said about turning down the music.

"Don't be ridiculous." Mom's getting mad. "That's not enough."

"I am not hungry," my sister says again, and she stares straight at Mom and turns the music up so loud her headphones make a buzzing noise. We're on the road now, and I can tell Mom's back is starting to cramp, turned around in her seat like that.

"I'll just leave them on the seat and you can have them later," she says loudly. "You can have them if you get hungry."

She sets the fries on the seat between Karen and me. Dad watches in the rearview mirror.

"I'll eat your fries," I say, reaching for them, hoping maybe it will shut everyone up. Karen yanks her headphones off her head and yells, "I don't want the goddamn fries!" And in a second she's rolled down the window and thrown the fries out. They hit the windshield of the car behind us and the driver leans on the horn, zooming past us. All four of the people inside give us the finger, even the little kid in the car seat, except he holds up the wrong finger. We watch the car go by, and Karen and I burst out laughing. Dad mumbles, "Nice, Karen. Very nice." He cranks up the air conditioning and the radio, not looking at Mom even though she's staring straight at him. After a second she goes back to her book, but not before she says, "Well you're eating when we get to the lake and that's the end of it."

We bite down on our tongues to stop laughing, because it's obvious that Dad's about to lose it.

4

The stairs up to the front door of the lake house are narrow, so we have to stand single file, Dad at the top of the stairs, jamming the key the realtor left under the worn mat in the lock over and over again. Mom's getting red behind him, saying, "Try it the other way. No, the other way!"

I stand behind her, sweating. Karen sits down on the bottom step, her headphones on, chin on her knees, scraping patterns in the dirt with a stick. We aren't even in the house yet and Mom and Dad are fighting.

"Joseph, let me try." Mom taps Dad's elbow with the tips of her fingers, and he shoves them away like she's burning him.

"No. It won't open."

He's sweating; it's running down the sides of his face, making a wet V down the back of his shirt. Karen looks up at me, rolls her eyes, and goes back to the stick and the dirt.

"Joseph, really, let me try."

Dad moves his body to block Mom's reaching arm, pulls off his T-shirt and wraps it around his fist. I never noticed how hairy his back was; it's all matted down with sweat. Nasty. If I ever get hair like that on my back, I'm shaving it off. Dad punches through a pane of glass, reaches his hand through, and unlocks the door from the inside. He pushes it open and makes a welcoming motion with his arm, "Come on in. Home sweet home."

Mom stalks past him, making a huge point of having to step over the shards of glass.

"Donnie, Karen, let's go. Inside."

I step one foot inside the door and Karen bumps into me from behind. Mom's standing in the kitchen with her hands over her mouth, looking hard at Dad, like she's asked him a question he hasn't answered yet. I don't know what's going on till I take a breath, or half a breath. I turn and run, pressing my hands over my mouth, my nose; even my eyes are stinging. Karen's got her tank top pulled up over her face, and we knock into Dad as we run past him and down the front steps. He stays on the top step, leaning his back against the railing and groaning, "Of course. Of course this would happen."

"Ack! What was it?" Karen's on her hands and knees, spitting in the grass. I'm stooped over doing the same.

"Something died. Something dead." I stick my tongue out, trying to get the air to lift the taste off.

Mom's on the steps with Dad. They lean against the banister, looking into the house. Mom nudges him with her elbow, saying softly, "Hey, it's all right. It's going to be fine."

He sighs in response and moves himself closer so they are just barely touching.

Karen rolls in the grass, making loud retching noises and grabbing her throat.

"What died? An elephant?" Karen rolls on her back. "How many?" She laughs. "An f'ing herd?"

I look at Mom and Dad for a moment more, then drop to the grass and roll, grabbing my throat. "Ack! What was it?" I give my high-pitched, squeaky imitation of Karen's voice. She squeals in mock anger and sends a handful of grass flying at my face. Mom and Dad give us one-and-a-half smiles and don't tell Karen to watch her mouth. At least that's something.

5

Mom takes a chance.

"This is silly. It's our first day of vacation and we're fighting."

She gives a pleading look to Karen, who's sulking in the back of the boat. Dad got the dead raccoon out from where it was rotting under the sink, but the house still needs airing out. So after eating leftover road-trip snacks out on the dock for an hour and not talking to each other, Mom made us all get in the rowboat. It's cooling down a little, even though the sun is still pretty high in the sky. It's quiet here and the air smells good. Mom looks at Dad, who's grunting every time he pulls the oars.

"How about you, muscle man? Don't you want to enjoy this? The beautiful lake, the clean air . . ." She gets the dreamy voice that's usually really annoying, and I don't want her to keep on embarrassing herself, so I say, "Yeah, let's not fight."

Mom shoots me this happy look that I can't help but return.

"Karen? Do you agree? No more fighting."

"Fine." Karen gets the word out as quickly as she can.

Mom looks at Dad. "Honey?"

He shrugs, but I see one side of his mouth twitching up.

"I ain't gonna stop fightin'," Dad says, with the horrible cowboy twang he used to use to make us laugh when we were little. "I aim to keep on fightin' till little miss there in the back of the boat tells us she's done fightin'."

"I said it!" Karen snaps. "I said I'd stop!"

"No, ma'am, you did not. You said 'Fine.'" He gives a spot-on imitation of Karen and she laughs before she can clamp her mouth shut to keep it in.

"I'll stop fighting," she says, trying to get her mad face back on.

Dad shrugs. "Can't hear ya."

"I'll stop fighting," Karen says louder.

"Speak up, girl. Your old pa can't hear nothin' since Cousin Vern set off them firecrackers next to his head."

"I'll stop fighting!" Karen half-yells.

"I think I heard somethin', but it sounded like a mosquiter to me. Ma? You hear anythin'?"

Mom grins and shakes her head.

Karen rolls her eyes, leans back in her seat, and yells, "I'll stop fighting!"

Her shout echoes back to us off the trees on the shore, and some guy walking his dog on the beach ducks like he's dodging a bullet and then looks side to side to see if anyone saw. We did, and we rock the boat with our laughter.

Mom says that from the air this lake looks like a gull flying. We row to the tip of each wing. There are houses all along the lake and as we row by, families—having cookouts on their porches or fishing off the docks—wave to us. We row by one old man in a canoe with his dog balanced in front. He calls out to Dad, "That's some hard work there!"

And Dad hollers back, "Yes, sir!"

The lake houses are mostly small, the size of the one we're staying in. We pass a small, sandy beach where some kids are having a campfire. Karen makes Dad row farther out into the lake, but she stares at the kids as we go by.

Across the lake from our house is Jake's, the general store. We row right up to it and tie the boat to the dock, all of us hungry and anxious to buy something to make dinner with back at the house. Jake's has wide plank floors and leaning shelves made from knobby wood. I can tell Mom loves it as soon as the screen door closes behind us because she gives a little squeal and an enthusiastic "Hello!" to the old man behind the counter.

Karen and I wander up and down the aisles, laughing at how everything is mixed together—lighter fluid next to bread, fishing line next to deodorant. Mom walks by us holding a box of pasta, looking puzzled and asking, "Have you seen any spaghetti sauce?"

The old man hears her and answers from the counter, "It's by the bug spray." Mom winks at us and whispers, "Of course it is."

When Mom and Dad are at the sloping counter paying for the stuff, the old man takes their money and says, "There's an ice cream stand round back, if you're interested." He winks at Karen. "It's where the young kids go to cause trouble." Karen forgives the wink and smiles at him.

When we're back outside, we all agree for once and decide that ice cream before dinner is the only way to go. It's mostly teenagers in line for ice cream or sitting at the half-dozen picnic tables in the grass. There's a dirt parking lot with a few parked cars, but it looks like most people get around by riding bikes. The sun is pretty much down now, and people are starting to swat at mosquitoes and put sweatshirts on over their swimsuits. Mom and Dad start talking to the only other adult in the ice cream line, a woman with white hair pulled back in a ponytail and a creaky black Lab lying at her side. Every time she moves up in line, the dog gets up slowly, takes a step, wags his tail once, and pretty much collapses again.

I study the board listing the ice cream flavors in pink and green chalk and feel the eyes of everyone else in line studying me. I plan to look at the chalkboard till it's our turn, because I'm sure as hell not going to look anyone in the eye.

Karen says, "I'm Karen, this is Donnie."

Karen's voice is almost challenging. And she nudges me with her elbow. I look down from the board and see all those eyes looking right at me. I croak out, "Hey."

A few kids just turn back around and ignore us, but a couple say hi. A few start asking Karen where we're staying, where we're from. I let her do all the talking.

We eat our ice cream on the dock so Dad doesn't have to row the boat with one hand, even though we all agree it'd be kind of funny to watch. The white-haired lady, Maddie, is coming back with us; she thanks us for saving Gustav the walk. She and Mom sit in the back of the boat and talk the whole way home. Karen and I sit up front with Gustav on our feet, dodging the water Dad keeps splashing at us with the oars.

6

Here's what our summer at the lake is like:

First of all, it's our summer, mine and Karen's and Amanda's. At first I thought they'd ditch me first chance they got, but they don't. We see other kids when we go to Jake's to sit on the picnic benches and make summertime conversation with whoever passes by, but Karen and Amanda never leave me for them. They never make me walk home and tell Mom they'll be home later. I keep waiting for it to happen, but it never does.

Our summer sounds like this:

Cannonball Let's row across the lake and get ice cream again Let's race rafts Who wants to play tag? Let's have an underwater breathing contest . . . I mean holding our breath contest I bet this house is haunted Let's take naps on the dock Marco! Let's put on a talent show Can you play duck-duck-goose with three people? Let's drop a watermelon on the dock from the porch and then eat it Polo! Donnie let me put the drops in your ears Let's play rummy I want another Popsicle Let's ask Maddie if we can take Gustav for a walk Who can do the most push-ups? Let's make a fire on the beach You've never had a s'more? Let's race I'll pull out that splinter for you Let's stay here forever.

It's like that; all summer. Only once is there a break in the momentum. Dad drives up with us, but he doesn't leave with us. He leaves in the middle of the summer. One Friday he and Mom come outside where we're on the porch, and he announces they are going back home for the weekend, and that Dad has to work for the rest of the summer. Work had called him, and they'd offered him a job at their new plant, the one that's an hour away from our house. They even got him an apartment down the street from the new plant, just for when he works late and can't make the drive home. Falling asleep while driving is really, really dangerous. I look at Karen, and see that Amanda is squeezing her hand. I know that something is happening, but since it's summer and we are happy, we all congratulate him and make him an enormous s'more and sing him "Happy Birthday" just because we feel like singing.

Maddie and Gustav come to stay with us for the night so Mom and Dad can drive home, and Maddie tells us ghost stories and makes Karen and Amanda cry by telling them about her husband who died.

When Mom comes back up the next day, Maddie meets her in the kitchen and gives her a long hug. Mom's shoulders shake and she lets out a long, shuddering sob. Karen looks at Amanda and then me and says, "I knew it. The bastard left us."

Mom gives a loud sniff and pulls away from Maddie. She wipes her eyes and says, "He did not leave us. Your father and I are just taking a little break. He's going to come home on weekends until we figure this out."

7

The walk around the lake has us sweating, and we run inside the lake house as the first raindrops fall fat and heavy on our heads. Karen pouts, looking out the window.

"No nap on the deck for us today. Let's play cards in Mom's room."

Mom's room used to be a porch, but it's been enclosed with three walls of windows. It has a wide bed with a white cover, and a ceiling fan, and we hang out there whenever it's raining. We sit on the bed and play round after round of gin. We eat chips, taking turns brushing the crumbs off the bed.

"Crap. I'm out," Karen says, tossing her cards on the bed. The rain has stopped. "I'm going to meet Mom on her walk with Maddie."

Karen and Mom are better together up here. They

barely fight, especially because Karen stopped saying "I'm not hungry" all the time and started eating with the rest of us.

Amanda deals.

We play a few more rounds.

"I'm sleepy," Amanda says, and she flops back on the bed, closing her eyes.

Kiss her, kiss her, kiss her. I don't. But I do lie down on the other end of the bed, facing her, the way we do every time it's raining, except this time Karen's not lying between us.

This is the best room I've ever been in. I force myself to close my eyes, peeking at Amanda every few seconds till I fall asleep. I wake up, and in her sleep she's stretched her arm out across the bed toward my hand, her wrist facing out. I can see its green-blue vein; I think I can see it pulse. I watch her shut eyes, reach out my fingers, and touch the pale skin of her wrist. Her eyelids flutter open and she looks at me for a moment and smiles, and then closes her eyes and falls back asleep.

The screen door slams and Karen calls, "Where are you guys?"

8

Things are going to be different in high school. I'm not going back to school the same kid I was in junior high. There's no way I'm going to spend the whole year getting run ragged by Chris and Bean. I let things go too far before school ended, I should have fought back right away. Whatever it was that started to happen with me and my friends last winter, it's going to end this fall.

Chris is the first one at what I guess will be our usual lunch table on the first day of school. He must have grown at least four inches over the summer, both up and out. He looks like a gym teacher or the guy who comes to clean out our septic tank. As I get closer to him, I see stubble on his chin. The first of his three sandwiches is already half eaten, and when I sit down at the table, he just looks at me and licks a blob of mayonnaise off his bottom lip.

"You missed some," I say, nodding toward his chin. He wipes at it with the back of his hand and looks over his shoulder at the kids streaming into the cafeteria.

"Where the hell is Bean?" he mumbles.

"How was your summer?" I ask, reaching into my lunch bag and finding not the sandwich I made this morning but the bag of carrots and celery Karen packed for herself. Great.

Chris shrugs and says, "All right." He starts in on the second sandwich, looking over his shoulder again and clearing his throat. I watch him ignore me while he chews, and I feel something like the flicker of a flame in my chest. I should just get up and walk away, say "Nice talking to you, asshole," and not look back. I don't do it, though. I stay sitting there, and when Bean sits down and keeps his eyes on Chris, I know he's waiting for Chris to give some sign about how they feel about me. And I sit there, waiting for the same thing. Maybe it's because it's the first day of school and he feels some kind of pity, or maybe because it's really hard to ignore someone who's sitting right in front of you, but Chris finally stops eating his sandwich long enough to ask, "How was your summer?" He sounds bored with the question and I know he'll be bored with my answer.

I think about not answering him, about letting his pity question just fall flat on the lunch table and leaving it there to rot.

"It was good. I went up to the lake with my friend Amanda."

That last part just pops out. I wanted to say something that would knock Chris out of his stupor, clear up that glazed look in his eyes.

"Your friend Amanda?" Chris drawls out the sentence, doing his best to sound disinterested.

"Yeah, who's Amaaaanda?" Bean asks, leaning over the table and laughing in my face.

I shrug and bite a piece of celery. God, she could at least put peanut butter on it. It's all stringy and I can feel it getting jammed up between my teeth.

I know the look Chris and Bean are giving me. They want me to say something they can laugh at. I suck on a string of celery between my teeth and mumble, "She's my friend . . ." Bean's mouth is twitching, waiting to laugh. "From Chicago."

"Chicago!" Bean's in hysterics, practically laughing himself under the table.

Chris laughs so hard he pretends to choke on his soda, and coughs out, "Yeah, they've got some hot girls in Chee-ca-goo."

I know there's nothing funny about Chicago. I know it wouldn't matter what I said. They just want to pick up where they left off last year.

"You do it with her?" Chris asks.

"Yeah, you do it with her at the laaaaake?" Bean squeals.

Then I have an entire conversation with Chris and Bean by doing nothing but laughing and shrugging and trying not to think about the fact I'm flailing deeper and deeper into a pit of lies. I wish I'd made up a name, I wish I hadn't said Amanda. Every time they ask me a question I force her face out of my mind. I try to forget the way she would sit next to me on the dock, our feet hanging in the water.

"You guys do it every day?"

"Five times a day?"

"I bet she liked it in the water."

"She was some sort of nympho, right?"

I just keep laughing and shrugging, half hoping that someone will change the subject and half hoping that we can talk about this every lunch period for the rest of my life. They're huddled around me, and even though I don't really say anything, we don't talk about anything else the whole time. By the time lunch is over, Chris and Bean think I spent the whole summer having sex twelve times a day with a girl named Amanda who had a thing for doing it in rowboats. I walk out of the cafeteria in something like slow motion, with Chris and Bean pressed in around me, still asking me questions and laughing at their own answers. It's a good first day back to school.

9

There is a message from Dad on the machine when I get home from school, just like there's been every Friday since we got back from the lake. And just like all the other Friday messages, this one says there's a problem at the plant and he can't come home this weekend, but next weekend he's definitely coming. It means we haven't seen him since he left the lake house this summer.

This whole first week of school Chris and Bean have hounded me for details about my Summer of Skanky Sex with Amanda. Every day, I think they'll be tired of thinking of new and disgusting questions to ask me about her, but they aren't. I still don't really say anything. I shrug my shoulders, shake my head, maybe laugh a little. Enough to keep them from ignoring me, but not enough to make me feel any guiltier than

I already do. Today when Bean launches into an Amanda story that is both nasty and physically impossible, I finally clam up. I don't shrug, or smile. I shut down and don't give them a thing to work from. They leave me sitting alone at the lunch table.

Even though Karen and Amanda have looked at the photographs a thousand times in the week since school started, they have been sprawled on their stomachs in the den all afternoon going through the pile of pictures we took at the lake. At every picture they squeal and laugh, sometimes even holding them up for a split second so I can see them from where I lie on the couch. I don't laugh with them, don't say a word, just glance over when they wave a picture in front of me. Since we've come back from the lake, since before school started even, I've lost my position as a point of our triangle. They're back to being a straight line, with no time or patience or interest in being part of any other geometric shape. They let me be near them, but if I make too much noise, make myself known, they get up and leave.

I watch Amanda flip through the pictures of our summer at the lake and wonder if she knows what we do together in my sleep. I stare at her and try to telepathically insert my thoughts into her head. So she's thinking, *Oh, look at this picture. Hey, wait a minute, you know who's really hot? Donnie. Donnie is really hot and I want to kiss him and let him feel me up.*

"Ohhhh. My God." Karen holds a photo up close to her

face "Look at that." She whips the picture under Amanda's nose. "Look, Amanda. Look at how huge my ass is!" Karen's almost breathless. "It's oozing out of my bathing suit!"

Amanda shrugs and rolls over onto her back, plants her palms on the floor, and pushes her pelvis up, stretching herself into a bridge, her shirt sliding up so I can see her belly and the very edge of her underwear. I watch her and try very hard not to lose my mind.

"God! Donnie, stop staring at us. You're so creepy . . ." Karen doesn't even look up from the picture when she says this.

Amanda drops back down to the floor and winks at me. I look into her eyes and think, *Take off your shirt, take off your shirt, take off your shirt.*

"Donnie! Go do your homework. Mom said." Karen jumps on the couch, knocking my legs off, her fingernails scratching my knuckles as she grabs the TV remote from my hand. It's Amanda's laughing that makes me knock Karen to the floor and sit on her stomach with her arms pinned by my knees on either side. I let drool hang out of my mouth and suck it back up before it hits her face. She's screaming at this point, and Amanda's a curled-up pretzel, laughing.

"Get OFF!"

The garage door opening makes the floor shake, and I slide off Karen, letting the last bit of spit land on the floor next to her face. I want to wink back at Amanda, but I can't because Karen's got my T-shirt pulled up over my head and she is trying to shove my face into her half-eaten bowl of ice cream. All I can think of is the zits on my back that came on after the summer, and how Amanda must be seeing the spray of nasty little white-tipped mountains on my skin. I shove Karen off, hard, and yank my T-shirt down in time to see Amanda putting on her jacket and saying hello to Mom and calling goodbye to Karen on the way out the front door. Karen's stomping upstairs, studying the rug burn on her elbow and calling me an asshole.

Mom yells at me for the ice cream on the rug, and Karen gets it for breaking the remote when she knocked it out my hand. Later on, when Karen's taking a bath, I take two photos from the pile on her desk. One is of Karen, Amanda, and me sitting at a picnic table behind Jake's, smiling at the camera. The other one is of Amanda standing on the edge of the dock, arms stretched above her head, ready to dive. That's the picture I tape up by my bed, just where the mattress hits the wall. Before I go to sleep, I stare at it in the dark.

10

I know right away something is wrong when I come home. Mom's car is in the driveway, and Karen's and Amanda's bikes are lying in the front yard, looking like they were ridden onto the lawn and dropped while they were still moving. When I walk in the house I can hear voices in the kitchen, and when I shut the door behind me, the voices stop.

Mom is standing with her hand on Amanda's shoulder. Amanda is sitting with her elbows on the table, and holding her head in her hands. Karen has her chair pulled up next to Amanda's, and the way they try to kill me with their eyes, I know right away what has happened. Nobody died. Yet. For a second they all just look at me and I just look at Amanda, and then Karen clenches her teeth and says, "I should kick your scrawny butt."

I do the first thing I think of. I smirk at her and say, "I'd like to see you try . . ." I glance at Amanda, who keeps her eyes on the kitchen table.

"Donnie, what were you thinking?" Mom has her I-just-can't-understand-you voice on. "Why would you start a rumor like that?"

I think about telling Mom to leave the room so the kids can talk.

I watch Amanda study the table and think, *Look at me, look at me, look at me.* She doesn't.

"Donald, a girl's reputation is—"

"Oh, for Christ's sake, Ma," Karen snaps.

"Don't swear at me, Karen. It's true. A girl's reputation is all she has."

Karen rolls her eyes and then levels them at me.

"Donnie, why'd you make up lies about Amanda?"

Amanda glances up at me with fierce but interested eyes. I shrug.

Amanda looks back at the table and Karen rails on.

"Did you think it'd make them like you? That's it, right? You wanted your loser friends to like you. Fucking pathetic—"

"Karen!" Mom snaps. "Watch your language!"

Karen ignores her, and as Karen talks, Mom just keeps making these little *meep* sounds in her throat every time Karen swears, like she wants to interrupt her but more than that she wants Karen to tear me a new butt hole.

"You know even the upperclassmen make fun of you

guys, right? You know that the only reason you don't get the shit [*meep*] beat out of you is because of me and Amanda, right? You care so much about what those fucking [*meep*] rejects think, you make up lies that nobody—*nobody*—in their right mind would believe. Seriously, Donnie. Did you think it wouldn't get back to us? Did you think someone would believe that you and *Amanda*—"

"Karen, that's enough," Mom says.

"I mean, she's a JUNIOR!" Karen finishes, shouting.

Mom says, "Amanda is too upset to even talk to you, Donnie."

"No I'm not, Mrs. LePlant. I'm just mad." Amanda sniffs and looks me full in the face. It was better when she was looking at the table. She wasn't lying when she said she was pissed off. I've never had someone look at me like that. *Look back down, look back down, look back down.*

"What happened, Donnie? Why'd you say those things about me?"

Karen jumps in. "Do you know what they're calling her, Donnie? Do you know what they wrote on her locker at school?"

I shrug.

"Rowboat."

I smile. I smiled! Oh, shit, I just smiled. I cough to try to cover it up, but Amanda is already across the kitchen and in my face.

"You think that's funny, Donnie? You think it's funny

that guys are taping pictures of their little brothers on my locker? It's only the second week of school and I have to deal with this shit!" She's so close I can feel her breath on my face. I could touch her lips with my tongue. "You think it's funny that they call me a cradle-robber and ask if I'm still breast-feeding? Yeah. Real funny, Donnie. Good one."

She hates me. She hates me so much; I can feel it coming out of her. Everything's gone wrong.

"I'm sorry," I mumble, and turn to walk out of the kitchen. She hates me; I'm the world's biggest jerk, fine. But I don't have to stand here and get reamed by her in front of my mom, for God's sake. But Amanda has other ideas. She moves in front me.

"You're right, you are sorry. You're a sorry little snot and you need to stay the hell away from me." She pokes me in the chest with her finger and it makes a hollow thump.

Amanda grabs her backpack off the floor and heads toward the door. She stops and turns around.

"You don't know what it's like, Donnie. I have to be on the defensive every day—just because some guys at school make a sport out of trying to feel you up in the hallways or listening to every word you say to see if they can turn it into something having to do with sex that they can shout out to their friends. It's exhausting, Donnie, and then you throw them a jewel like this and they practically pee themselves with excitement."

The sound of Amanda slamming the sliding glass door

stays in the room for a long, long time. Then Mom says, "They try to feel you up in the hallways?"

Karen says, "For Christ's sake, Ma," and pushes past me out of the kitchen.

Mom says, *Meep.*

11

I'm on the couch when Mom and Karen get home. There's a marathon of kung fu movies on cable that I've been watching since I came home from school. I was hoping Karen and Mom would be gone long enough for me to watch them till my brain melted and nothing mattered anymore.

Across town, Chris and Bean are watching the same thing. I should be with them, they even invited me, the first time they've asked me to hang out since school started, but instead I'm home. Alone. Because Dad is trying to ruin my life.

Karen comes in first and runs past me and up the stairs—*thud, thud, thud* SLAM! I can hear her start to wail before the bedsprings sink under her.

Mom's slow up the front stairs. One step. Rest. Next step. Rest. She drops her bags at the top of the stairs and leaves them there, puts the teakettle on before she even takes off her coat. I've stopped watching TV and am waiting to see what happens. Karen's wailing upstairs, and I can hear her smacking her minibasketball against the headboard of her bed, making new little dents for Mom to freak out about. I turn off the TV and listen to the teakettle boil, the ball smack against the wood. I don't make a sound. I'm almost not even here.

"Donnie."

Mom catches me right as I'm about to float out the window. I get up and stand in the doorway of the kitchen. She's taken off her coat, left it hanging inside out on the back of a chair. She's resting her head in the palm of her hand, I can see it's heavy. She gives me a tired smile.

"How was your afternoon with your dad?"

I don't know how to answer this, so I don't. When the third week of school started and he still hadn't come home ("Big problem at the plant, kids. Next weekend, I promise." BEEEEP), Mom called him and yelled at him and he said he was going to come after school today to see me. I stand in front of my mom, feeling heat rise up to my face. I should have lied and said he'd come, but I think of it too late. She's already getting furious. It's embarrassing, knowing that she's going to call him, that she has to yell at him to guilt him into coming to see me.

Mom leaves a message on Dad's machine. She ends with, "This is not what we agreed on. This is not what we discussed.

The pieces of his heart can only break down so much; you are crushing them into dust. You are giving our son a heart of dust."

She slams the phone down, twice. I leave the room before she can give me her *I'm sorry* hug, my consolation prize for being a loser.

I tap with one finger on Karen's door and listen. She stops throwing the ball and says, "What."

"It's me," I say, wishing I had a more convincing argument for her to let me in.

"Go away."

Again with the basketball. *Thud, thud thud.*

"Dad didn't come today."

The ball stops again, the bed creaks as she rolls off, and she opens up the door a crack. Her face is splotchy, puffy.

"That sucks." She sniffs. "Did he call?"

I shake my head. Karen opens the door farther and pulls me inside by my shirt, closing the door behind us. She's been ignoring me since the whole doing-it-with-Amanda incident last week.

"Dad's become an asshole. Don't you ever get like that Donnie, don't you ever be an asshole."

I'm still not sure how I actually got into Karen's room, so I just nod. She studies my face.

"Donnie, you should ditch those kids you hang out with."

I look at her.

"I mean, Donnie, do you even like them?"

I shrug, racking my brain for a way to keep her talking, a way to keep her from kicking me out.

"Now get out, I don't want Mom coming up here. She's an A-hole too."

I nod as Karen reaches behind me, opens the door, and backs me out of the room.

Mom's coming up the stairs, and Karen's face starts to get splotchy again, her eyes narrow.

"Mom, I told you I don't want to talk about it."

She says this before Mom's even at the top of the stairs.

"Karen, I don't understand what you're so upset about. So she said that you were—"

"MOM!" Karen's shriek makes both Mom and me jump, and the slam of her door makes us both step back.

"Donnie, please go put water on for pasta," Mom says.

Karen's door swings open and her red face juts out. "I am not eating any goddamn pasta!"

"Karen, this is ridiculous. You're not fat. Ms. Stephans was just trying to . . ."

"To what? What, Ma? What was she trying to do? She called me FAT!"

"She did not call you fat. She called you curvy."

Karen slams the door again, and Mom says the rest of her sentence to the hinges, "There's a difference."

Karen opens her door a crack and presses through the narrow opening. Her eyes are wild.

"I'm not going to school tomorrow. I can't see those

girls. I can't let them see me. Mom, you can't make me go. I'll die. I'll die if I have to go. I want to change schools. I want to go to school with Cousin Bobby in Chicago. School just started, I won't have missed too much. Mom, don't make me go to school. Don't ever tell anyone what that teacher said about me, don't ever tell anyone. Promise me, okay? Promise me you won't ever tell anyone what that woman said? Because it's not going to be true anymore. I'm not going to let it be true anymore."

Mom gently pushes open the door, reaches to take Karen by the hand. She leads her past me into the bathroom.

"Sssshhh now. You need to calm down, Karen. You need to calm down now."

"Promise me first, Mom."

They close the door to the bathroom. The faucet turns on for a moment, and then off again. Mom's going to wet a washcloth and put it behind Karen's neck. I listen at the door.

"Promise you what? Cousin Bobby isn't even in high school anymore. They finally graduated him and he's going to community college. And no, you can't go to college with him."

"Momma, don't make me go to school tomorrow. I want to stay home. I have to stay home."

"We'll see how you feel in the morning."

A faucet is turned on again and I can't hear what Karen says.

I don't turn the stove on under the pasta pot. I can tell Mom and Karen are in it for the long haul. So I put the pot of water on the stove and do a crossword puzzle at the table, listening for signs of them stopping.

When Amanda comes into the kitchen, I know that Mom has called in the big guns. In the past few days I've felt Amanda's anger at me cooling. I could tell it was more of an effort for her to ignore me the way Karen did. I think about telling her that sleeping with her, even if I just made it up, only made me popular for half a second. I'm back to being the kicked bucket.

She sits across the table from me.

"How is she?"

I shrug and look hard at the newspaper. Amanda moves to get up, and I ask, "So why's she's freaking out?"

"It's so dumb," Amanda says quickly, sitting back down. "Karen's so frigging dramatic. I can't believe your mom called me to help calm her down. Karen's going to lose it when she finds out."

"So what happened?" I ask again.

"We got our gym uniforms today, and Ms. Stephans had us all in the locker room trying them on. She was making everyone stand in front of her so she could make sure we're not wearing them too tight or too loose, and when it was Karen's turn, she said, 'If you're lucky enough to be as curvy as Karen here, you can go a size up.'"

"So?" I say, but I think that maybe Karen's like me. Maybe she's happiest when she's slipping through a crowd. Maybe she knows the same thing I do, that nobody can bother you if they don't know you're there. My stomach lurches when I think about how it must have felt, to think you're invisible, and suddenly have all those eyes looking at you, instead of looking right through you.

"So," Amanda says, like I've missed something really obvious, "Ms. Stephans sucks, and Karen's a freak about her weight. She thinks she's fat. She keeps going on diets. Don't tell her I told you. I'm going upstairs. Karen's going to freak."

12

Dad surprised us by coming home for the weekend. He actually scared the crap out of Mom when he came in, because he came up the back porch, through the sliding glass door, and into the kitchen. Mom was doing dishes and caught his reflection in the window over the sink. She screamed and spun around, ready to crack his head open with a soapy pan. By the time Karen and I ran into the kitchen, Dad had pulled Mom into a hug and taken the pan out of her grip. Mom was saying in a shaky voice, "You said on the message you weren't coming home."

"Do I need an appointment to come to my own house?" Dad asked softly. "Well then, get your calendar, go to today, October second, and write 'Dad's coming home,'" Dad said, and I could hear how he was trying to keep his voice friendly.

"Kids, go on into the living room and let your mother and I talk for a minute."

Karen didn't move, so neither did I. She looked at Mom till Mom said, "Go on now."

Then she turned and walked out, and I followed.

When they came out of the kitchen, Mom declared a family fun night. Seriously, she said, "I declare a family fun night!" It's so obvious this is all about Dad. There's no way we couldn't hear him and his grumbly whine when they were in the kitchen, annoyed that we hadn't planned a night of board games and heart-to-heart talks for him. We didn't even know he was coming home. Asshole. Knowing he put Mom up to this, making her be the jerk that has to fake enthusiasm, Karen and I both make a (sort of) big deal about being excited. I hate to see Mom like this. She's like an open wound waiting for salt.

Tonight "family fun night" means watching TV together, which differentiates it from every other night only because Dad's here. A commercial comes on for a chain of ice cream places.

"Don't we have stuff for sundaes?" Dad asks.

Karen and I lock eyes. You might think he was talking about ice cream. But we know that what he just said loosely translates into: "You are a rotten wife and you deprive your family of love by not keeping sweetened dairy products ready to serve at all times."

"We did, but we don't anymore," Mom says. Translation:

"Shut the hell up, you thankless bastard. Were you not here for the 'family fun night' declaration?"

"It'd be nice. Sundaes," Dad says, like it's a deep thought, "Especially for *family fun night*."

Why'd he have to emphasize that last part?

"Well, let's go out and get some," Mom says, standing up, trying to stifle one of her tired sighs. "Friendly's is still open."

We all know Dad won't go for it. It'd be too easy.

"I'm not going to Friendly's with you," Karen says. I glare at her. She shrugs. She's not helping.

"We'll get take out," Mom says, holding a hand out toward Karen. "No one will see you with your horrible, embarrassing parents."

"Why don't we just make them here?" Dad says this like it is the most reasonable thing anyone's said all night.

"I told you, we don't have the stuff to make them," Mom snaps, giving up on Karen and pulling me up off the couch by my arm. She tells me to get my coat.

"Why not?" Dad asks.

It's like seeing two cars slide on ice, knowing they're going to collide, and all you can do is watch.

"Why not?" he asks again.

"You're honestly asking me why we don't have ice cream sundaes at our house?" Mom puts all her effort into sounding incredulous.

"Yes," Dad says, and then, "Sit down, Karen," when he

catches her standing up and heading toward the stairs. Karen tried to make her exit too early. Maybe he's been gone so long she forgot the rules. We have to wait till they're so into tearing each other apart that they don't notice us leave.

"Why don't you go make yourself brownies or Popsicles or popcorn, or any of the other five hundred billion things we have to eat in the house?" Mom's voice is almost at fight volume.

"I just don't understand why we had stuff for sundaes and now we don't." Dad has a fight voice too, except it's the opposite of Mom's. He keeps his as quiet and calm as possible. It means that if Mom's voice raises above a whisper when they fight, she sounds like a raving lunatic.

The rage in Mom's eyes tells us we're free to go. Karen grabs her coat and heads for the front door, for Amanda's. I watch her walk out and then I go upstairs and lie on my stomach in the hallway outside of my bedroom so I can see through the space between the railing. It's warmer than the stoop would be, and it's not like Karen would sit out there with me anyway.

"Because!" Mom's so mad she's shaking. "Because I bought all the stuff for sundaes three weeks ago, when you were supposed to come home and you didn't. So, since then Karen and Amanda ate all the cherries and got bellyaches, the bananas went bad, Donnie ate the ice cream, and I dropped the goddamn jar of chocolate sauce and it broke."

"We could have gotten more," Dad says. I can't see his face from where I sit, but I can hear he is full on into a man-pout.

"Goddamn it!" Mom yells. "Why do you do this? Isn't it enough that you've got us all here tonight! Why do you have to ruin every attempt I make to pull this family together? Watch the movie! Enjoy that fact that you are here and you are with your family! You can't make us be like those families you used to watch on TV! I know that's what you want, but that's not real life, and I can't give that to you! These ideas you have about what a family should be, you hinged them on the wrong person, buddy. I didn't sign on for this."

She starts pacing around the room, straightening up and slamming things. "That's not what I want for my life. I don't want my sole purpose to be making sure there's chocolate sauce and ice cream, or to take some satisfaction in the way laundry smells when it's done. My sister Janice and I worked ourselves to the bone cleaning up after Daddy when Mom died. I lived that life once, and I don't want to do it again, and yet . . . here I am."

Mom looks around like she's been brought here against her will.

"Well I'm sorry I didn't have a 'real' family when I was a kid," Dad says. "I'm sorry all I had was television to show me what a family should be, and I'm sorry you feel so trapped in our life."

Dad had a weird sort of growing up. His mom and dad died when he was eight, and there was no one to take him in except for his grandmother. She lived in an old folks home, just for women. They let him move in as a special exception, so he grew up surrounded by old ladies. I think it seriously messed him up.

"If I'd had a real family," he says quietly, "I'd know how to be a real father and not drive my own children out of the room every time I come home."

"You are a real father." Mom sits next to Dad on the couch, touching him on his arm. "I don't know why you can't just be real with them."

"What is that?" Dad asks, leaning away from Mom. "To be real? What do I teach them? How to clean dentures and play bridge? There's nothing I can teach them."

Mom folds her hands in her lap and thinks for a moment. She says in a slow, soft voice, "It's sad you didn't know your dad, it's terrible they put you in that place with those old women, but that doesn't mean that you can't learn. Why don't you even try? Can't you just try?"

13

Mom tells us during breakfast. She waits till we both have our mouths full of cereal, and says, "Guess what? Your dad's coming home for the day." I look at Karen and see that, like me, she's frozen midchew. Dad hasn't been home since what Karen and I secretly refer to as the Family Fun Night Massacre. We just turned to the November page on the calendar. But we've been talking to him on the phone every few days since it happened. Karen's started to refer to him as Phone-Dad and keeps her conversations with him short and snappy, until the end when I can tell he's said he loves her, and Karen goes silent and then mumbles, "I know you do. Me too," and holds the phone out toward me saying, "It's Phone-Dad." I don't care if our conversations are short or if he asks different combinations of the same five questions every time, I'm just glad he calls at all.

Karen manages to swallow her mouthful of sugar-free, fat-free, taste-free cereal and asks, "He said that? He said he's coming today?"

Mom gives an overly enthusiastic nod in response and starts to clear the table.

"Interesting," Karen says, raising her eyebrows at me. I look at her and think, *Shut up shut up shut up.* She won't ever give him a chance. He's been gone so long, and she's going to ruin it before he even gets here.

"So, Mom," Karen continues in the voice she uses when she wants to sound like a really mature, really reasonable person, "why is he coming home?"

Mom gives what's meant to be a happy shrug in response, but I can tell she's stopped breathing.

"I mean,"—*shut up shut up shut up*—"do you really want him to come over? Can't we just keep Phone-Dad instead?" Karen's starting to laugh out loud. "That way we can just hang up on him when—"

Mom's hand shoots out over the table. For a second I think she is going to slap Karen, but instead she cups Karen's chin in her hand and stares hard into her face. It actually shuts Karen up for a second.

"Karen," Mom says, "this is the part where we all try really, really hard to keep our family together."

Karen pulls her face away from Mom's hand and gives a fake laugh.

"God, Mom. I know that. I was just joking."

"Well, your jokes hurt. He's still your dad."

"If you say so," Karen mumbles, trying to give me a conspiratorial smile.

I ignore her and watch as Mom bursts into tears. Karen goes pale and rushes to where Mom is standing with her arms straight by her sides, her head down and her hair hanging over her face. Karen crouches down a little so she is looking up into Mom's face, saying, "I'm sorry, Mom. I didn't mean it. Mom, I'm really sorry."

Mom just keeps shaking her head, looking at the ground. Karen pleads what I am thinking, "Oh God, Mom, please look up. Look at me, Mom." Karen carefully lifts Mom's chin with her fingers till Mom's red face is staring at us both. I don't realize I was holding my breath till I exhale. I'm so relieved that it's still her face. I was terrified that it had turned into something else. I wish I could get up from the table. I wish I could . . . participate. I'm rigid, my joints are soldered in this position. I manage to wrench open my jaw and say, "You made her cry."

Karen scowls at me.

"You're going to ruin—" My voice is a growl, but before I can finish my sentence, Mom says in a shaky voice, "You kids . . ." Mom sputters, "You need to know that just because your Dad and I are taking a break from each other, doesn't mean we're taking a break from loving you."

That's it. I'm done. I get up and leave them in the kitchen. I don't need to sit here and listen to them making things real.

• • •

When Dad gets here, Mom has us sit in the living room. I understand. We can't be in the den because then we could watch TV and ignore each other until we found something to fight about. We can't be in the kitchen because either Karen would start complaining that all we ever eat is "fat food" or Dad would start rifling through the fridge, and we'd have the Family Fun Night Massacre, Part 2: I Thought You Bought Cheese Dip. So we sit in the living room because it's the only room in the house our family hasn't broken up in. Yet.

It's not going well. Dad's sitting in an armchair facing the couch where I sit wedged between Mom and Karen. Dad's asking Karen and me careful questions, and we keep our answers short and smooth—with nothing to snag there's less chance of a fight. Dad's running out of ways to ask us how school is, and since he already told us work was "too busy," and since it'd be too weird to ask him about his apartment or what he does at night or if he has cable or eats pizza Friday nights like we used to together, we don't ask anything. The silences between his questions get longer and longer, and Mom hasn't said a word because I think this visit is supposed to be about Karen and me and Dad. I can feel that everyone is about to scatter and I know it's up to me to stop them from bolting from the living room. We are standing on the edge of a cliff, looking at swirling, rolling water below. Behind us is a fire that will soon engulf us, and in front of us is a long drop that we may not survive. I know the fire will kill us, but there's a chance we could survive the fall.

I look at Dad, who is starting to get up from the armchair with his eyes on the door, and I say to myself, *I'm going in.*

I open my mouth and I talk nonstop for seventy-one minutes. It's a little sloppy at first, but at least Dad sits back down. I'm aware that I'm telling four stories at the same time, and that Mom and Karen and Dad are all starting to look at each other and laugh because this is how I used to be when I was kid—the second anyone gave me any sort of attention, I'd start in on a story about my pet elephant or how I captured the tooth fairy in my clothes hamper, and I'd talk till I ran out of things to say or Karen put her hand over my mouth. It's the same thing now—if I can keep talking, they'll keep listening. They'll stay. I narrow in on one story at a time, and for over an hour they hear about secret service agents lost in the woods, about tightrope walking champions, about kung fu masters and specialized firefighters that dash in and out of burning buildings rescuing kids. As I talk, I watch it get dark outside, and see a light early-November snow turn into a freak early-November blizzard. I watch Dad lean back in the chair and relax. I watch his eyes saying things to Mom, and her eyes answering. I watch Karen as she tucks her feet under her and curls against the arm of the couch, her arms folded in front of her and a happy look on her face. I watch my reflection in the window, and know that I am looking at a hero. I'm the one that's saving us all.

At seven thirty P.M. Karen exchanges a glance with Mom and sits up, saying, "Mom, I'm starved. Can we eat?" I'm grateful.

My throat is sore, my stomach is growling, and I'm not even sure what I'm saying anymore. I've kept Dad here so long that the snow has piled too deep for him to leave, and he'll have to stay overnight for the first time since before we left for the lake house last summer. The rest of the night passes quietly. We eat together, watch TV together, and I go to sleep feeling like a final puzzle piece has been clicked into place. In the middle of the night I get up and look over the upstairs railing into the den below. Karen tiptoes out of her room and stands next to me. We are looking for the same thing, but I know we are wishing for opposites. Karen looks down into the den and gives a triumphant look in response to my frown. Dad is sleeping on the couch. Mom is still sleeping alone. I raise my chin. I don't care. I still saved us, even if for just a little while.

The next morning Karen and Amanda are under blankets in the den watching talk shows, which means I'm in the den watching Amanda watch talk shows. As soon as the TV announced that school was canceled this morning, Amanda crossed the street through two feet of snow, wearing her pajamas and slippers under her snowboots and winter coat. She and Karen have plans for an all-day UnSlumber Party, and since it's daytime, they can't kick me out of the den. I'm ready to tell them, "It's my den too!"

Dad's been up since before it was even light out, swearing at the snowblower in the driveway. Mom's in the kitchen talking on the phone to either Aunt Janice or Maddie from the lake, saying, "I told him he should have come home some-time this fall and gotten that stupid snowblower ready for the winter."

A commercial comes on, and Karen gets up and stretches, glancing out the window.

"Oh, my God!" She runs over to the window. "Amanda, come look at this!"

"God, it's so weird," Amanda says, standing next to Karen.

"What?" I ask, and look between them out the window. Our dads are crouched over our snowblower. Amanda's dad's explaining something involving a wrench.

"Amanda," Karen says in an awed voice, "you realize this is really the first time they've even talked? I can tell by the way he's holding that wrench that your dad, like, loves my dad."

Amanda nods in agreement. "Your dad's like the son he never had."

"Maybe they'll start going on man dates," Karen says, "like ice fishing. Your dad can show mine how to shoot bears or chew tobacco."

Amanda laughs. "My dad doesn't shoot bears. He hasn't been hunting since we moved here. I bet they'll just talk about carburetors and hot-water heaters."

"Man dates are next," Karen says, shaking her head.

"When you think about it, it'd be kind of sweet."

"What?" Karen laughs. "For our dads to be platonic lovers? If they got married we could be sisters."

"Well, I mean, your dad didn't have a dad, right? And my dad didn't have a son, so there." Amanda gives a satisfied smile. "They'll fill up holes in each other's lives."

"I guess." Karen looks at me. "Maybe Dad will teach you some of that manly-man stuff, Donnie."

I shrug. Part of me hopes he'll start getting Amanda's dad to teach him stuff so he can teach me and not feel like such a failure. And part of me thinks he'd rather just have a dad than be one. Great, this means I have to grow up and find some burly dude to be my pseudofather and teach me how to change oil and grill steak. I shake my head and feel Karen's and Amanda's eyes on me.

"Let's go pajama sledding!" Karen says. "Donnie, get your pj's on, you're coming too."

Sometimes, it's like it was at the lake.

14

It's taken a week for the snow to melt, and now everything is a slushy, icy mess. My ears started hurting yesterday, and since then I've spent all of school resting my head on whatever table I'm sitting at. The good part is that my ears are so filled up with gunk that I can barely hear my teachers. Today at lunch Bean poked me in the side and said, "What's wrong with you?" because I was too worn out to defend myself against whatever bullshit he and Chris were saying about me. I didn't answer, so they got up and left me in the cafeteria. The lunch lady had to wake me up so she could wash the table.

I manage to duck Mom after school and almost all night, till I pass her coming out of the bathroom. I can tell she's stopped walking once she's passed me. I almost make it to my room before she says, "Donnie, come here for a minute."

I hate how there's no doubt for her that I'll come when I'm called. I go in my room and close the door.

"I know there's a boy with a fever in there!" Mom says through the door, knocking.

Since dinner my skin has been heating up, becoming too tight on my body. She thinks just because she gave birth to me she can sense any time I'm sick.

"Donald LePlant, you know I can sense these things. Open up and let me take your temperature."

I call out from where I've flopped on my bed, "If you know I have a fever, why do you have to take my temperature?"

"Now I *know* you have a fever, because you only talk back when you're temperature's above a hundred and two. Open the door."

I don't answer. I hate how Karen can swear at Mom, slam the door in her face, ignore her for days at a time, but the moment I ask a legitimate question, I'm "talking back."

"Do you want to have to go to the ER tomorrow?" she asks. "Because you know that's what will happen if you don't take medicine tonight. Remember last time? You wouldn't let me get near you, and you ended up with a double infection, and we spent all night in the emergency room. You missed two days of school and, you know, I think that's why you got a D in earth science last year."

If she'd just let me keep my own medicine, not dole it out to me like I'm a drooling idiot-five-year-old, then I could take care of this myself.

"Earth science can kiss my ass!" I yell, and I hear Mom smother a laugh. I get up, open the door, and say, "It's not funny!"

She makes a serious face and nods, but I can tell she's still laughing at me with her eyes. She loves making a fool out of me. I start to the shut the door. She holds it open with her hand.

"Wait, wait, Donnie, I'm sorry. It's just so rare I get a rise out of you. Karen tells me every other minute the ways I'm ruining her life, but you, you wait till you can't control your mouth to say anything apart from 'yes' or 'no' or 'fine' or 'good.' It's just . . . funny. Can I please feel your forehead now?"

I tip my head out the door so she can press her hand against my face. She squints her eyes and tips her head to the side, holding her breath. Mom thinks feeling for a fever is a talent, but I'm so hot I bet I have that wavy hot-pavement vapor coming off my head. She pulls her hand away and says, "I knew it!" There's no way to argue with her now. She felt the proof in the palm of her hand. I open my bedroom door all the way and fling myself face down on my bed while she starts clomping around, cleaning my room, and giving her whole Western-medicine-has-destroyed-my-son monologue. She doesn't stop talking, even when she goes into her bathroom to get my medicine or when she manages to change the sheets while I'm lying on my bed. She's swearing about how she can't believe she has to put me on antibiotics again and she never should have let my doctor put me on such heavy medication when I was just a baby. She says it made the ear infections come back stronger, so the drugs had to be stronger, and now they've got us over a G-D barrel scaring her to death, saying if I don't take the medicine then I'll become profoundly deaf.

When she's done shoving clothes into drawers, slamming the drawers shut, and lining my shoes up in the closet, she says, "There," and immediately launches into her other favorite monologue, which is about how a sick person in a messy room makes her want to scream. It reminds her of when her granddad got sick and nobody knew, and when she and Aunt Janice went to visit one day, he was laid up in bed and his house was filled with garbage, and she thinks that's why he didn't get better, that's why he died.

Mom gives me my medicine, pulls the covers up to my chin, shuts off the light, and closes the door, almost all the way. She sticks her head back in my room and says, "No son of mine is going to a be pill-popping antibiotic junkie buried up to his neck in a messy room. Sleep tight." She closes the door behind her.

"The movie was fine. I'm really tired."

I wake up and look at the clock. I've slept for an hour. I listen for Amanda's voice in the hall but hear only Karen saying, "Amanda went home and I'm going to bed. Night, Mom."

"Okay, good night. Don't wake your brother, he's got an ear infection."

I hear Karen snort. "What else is new?"

I think I fall asleep again, just for a second. I wake up because I hear Mom open her own bedroom door and tap softly on Karen's.

"Karen, you have to see the little snowman I got for Aunt Janice . . ." I hear her turn Karen's doorknob, open the door, and scream.

"JESUS! My God . . ."

I'm standing in the hall before I realize I've jumped from my bed and run out of my room.

Mom's staring at Karen's closed door, her hands over her ears. Dad's coming out of their bedroom. When did he come home?

"What the hell are you doing here?" I ask him, and realize that I still have a fever.

I laugh at the stupid offended look on his face. After a second he says, "Oh. Your mom mentioned you weren't feeling well."

I do an equation in my head. Fever equals the right to say whatever the hell I want. I should call Chris and Bean and scream insults at them until they disintegrate. But first I should say something else to Dad. I try to think of something that will really knock him down. Or maybe I could actually just knock him down with superhuman fever strength.

"Joseph, she's as thin as a rail!"

Mom's ruining my moment by banging with her palm on Karen's door. Dad rolls his eyes and leans down close to Mom, like she's a child speaking too softly for him to hear.

"What now? What happened?" he asks.

"Joseph!" Mom screams. "She's so skinny you can see her bones! Karen! Open up!"

She bangs more with her fist and frantically rattles the door handle. All I can think of is the tapeworms we studied in science, how they get inside you, eat your food, and grow bigger while you get skinnier and skinnier. How you have to take them out by twirling them around a ruler, straight out of your stomach.

"Oh, God, what do we do? Joseph?"

"Get a ruler!" I yell. I know why they don't listen. They think it's the fever talking. Little do they know the fever has opened up stores of genius no one ever knew I had.

Dad hates it when Mom gets "excited."

"Don't get excited, Diane," he says.

"Don't be a dickhead, Dad," I say. They both ignore me. Long live my fever!

He steps closer to Karen's door.

"Karen!" He barks. "Come out here. Now. Karen!"

Mom makes fists with her hands and holds them up against her mouth. She looks at Dad with wide eyes.

"Maybe we should call the police," Mom whispers.

Dad snaps his head back to glare at her. I make siren noises that ricochet around us, echoing off the walls.

"Oh, for God's sake, Diane," Dad says over my sirens, "why would we call the police? What would we tell them?"

Mom shakes her head. "I don't know, Joseph, I just thought . . ."

"We don't need the police to get our daughter out of her room, Diane."

"Yeah, *Diane*!" I say. They ignore me. Maybe I'm actually still asleep in bed, and this is a fever dream.

"Karen!" Dad yells. "Step away from the door. . . ."

"Oh, for God's sake, Joseph!"

"I'm going to kick it in!"

This makes me laugh, loud and long.

"Damn it, Donnie," Mom yells, finally looking at me. "Go back to bed!" She turns to Dad. "Joseph, your knee! Karen! Open the door before your dad pops his knee!"

I start to laugh again till I see how Mom grabs at Dad's arm as he kicks the door twice. I jump at the sound, all the laughter sucked out of me. The doorjamb makes a sharp cracking sound as it splits, and I cover my head with my hands and hum. *Hummmmmmmmm*. The second kick opens the door, and I think they'll both rush in like cops, but they just hover in the hall, peering in at Karen. She's in bed, lights off, covers up to her chin, trying to look undisturbed by the fact that her door is hanging by one hinge and the harsh light of the hall is glaring on her face.

"Karen, we know you're awake. Get up." Dad finally steps into her room, switches on the light, and stands with his hands on his hips at the foot of her bed. "Your mother says you're too skinny. Sit up so I can see you."

"Joseph!" Mom's hands are pushed out toward Dad, trying to catch the words as they fly out of his mouth. "You don't . . . Why would you say that!"

Karen still lies with her eyes closed, although now her jaw is set tight so that it pulses on the side of her face. Dad looks calmly from Mom to Karen. His words are slow, quiet, measured.

"We need to not get hysterical here. We need to discuss what is happening. You need to let me—"

Mom interrupts and asks him, "Do we take her to the hospital?"

"To the hospital?"

"Well, I don't know!"

For the first time Dad sounds a little unsure of himself. "Is that what you do? Take her to the hospital?"

"I don't know . . . ," Mom whispers. "She's so small, you didn't see her. The way her skin is . . ."

Karen sits up, making a shadow on the wall. She swings her legs over the side of the bed and looks squarely at my parents.

"Don't talk about me like I'm not here. I'm fine. I've been stressed out over my science test. That's all. It's all over now, I took the test today." She stands up and turns, like she's going to close what's left of the door and go back to sleep. She looks like she is how she always is, annoyed. But she can't pull it off, because a second after she stands up, she crumples down onto the floor.

.   .   .

"Hello," I say, and my voice comes out a raspy squeak. I say it again louder, "Hello," and the word gets swallowed up by the sound an empty house makes. They have been at the emergency room for two hours with Karen, and I have been sitting here, straight-backed on the edge of the middle couch cushion, for one hour and fifty-four minutes.

When you're alone like this, time will show you its tricks. Like taking four minutes to click from one thirty-four A.M. to one thirty-five A.M. Or moving from two A.M. to two thirteen A.M. when you swear you just looked down and scratched your ankle for a millisecond.

I say, "Ha!" when the clock does that last trick.

You can't argue with a clock. Time can mess with you as much as it wants. I still have a fever. Without touching them, I try to feel what my ears are feeling.

Any infection in there? I think.

"No," they answer back, like naughty kids. "No one here but us ears!"

Definitely a fever. I'm going to take more medicine.

"No!" screams the empty house, and the clock, and my ears. "You've sat here for one hour and fifty-nine minutes, and you can't get up now. Besides," they all chant, "there are ghosts in the house. Better sit here with us where you're safe. If you look in the mirror in the bathroom, you are going to see behind you the rotting face of a corpse. You'll look it in the eyes and it will scare you to death."

"Well," I say, "if you say so. You can't argue with a fever."

"Or time," the clock says with an attitude.

I sit still for one more moment, then jump up and run to the bathroom before they can stop me. I don't look in the mirror when I open it, I just take out the medicine and swallow two pills without water. When I close the mirror, though, I look into it, and I see the rotting-face man. His skin is gray and half-eaten. It hangs off in patches. He's wearing a really nice suit.

"Hello," I say.

He says, "Ugggghhhh."

"Well," I say. "I'd better get back. You know how the clock gets."

"Ugggghhhh." He nods in agreement and what's left of his nose falls off. I leave him to find it, and I go back to the couch. The clock and the house and my ears are not speaking to me.

"Fine," I say. "Be that way." And I lie down on the couch.

"His fever must have broken. He sweat through his shirt. Donnie . . . Donnie . . . We're back."

I wake up, curled in a ball at one end of the couch. My shirt's sticking to my back, but my fever is gone.

"Hey," I say. "What happened?" Dad is kneeling down next to me, his hand on my forehead.

"You're not warm now. And you're not swearing at me, so you must be feeling better. Some night, eh?"

I nod. "What happened with Karen?"

"Go change, and we'll tell you at breakfast."

They are all at the table when I come back downstairs. Karen keeps trying to bite off the plastic bracelet they gave her at the ER, until Mom gives her a pair of scissors. Karen, Mom, and Dad look exhausted, but not unhappy.

"What happened?" I say, sitting in my place. Mom puts a plate of eggs in front of me.

"Your sister," she says, with a sharp look at Karen, "let herself get stressed out about school, got herself dehydrated, and didn't give herself time enough to eat."

"I aced my test, though," Karen says, swallowing egg.

"What did they do to you?" I ask Karen. Dad pours Mom coffee, and she gives him a small smile.

Karen shrugs. Dad says, "They hydrated her with an IV."

Karen sticks out her arm to show me the Band-Aid with a cotton ball under it.

"The important thing," Mom says, sitting down, "is that now Karen knows not to push herself like that. Right?"

Karen nods obediently.

"Well," Mom says with a look around the table, "I don't know when the last time we all sat down to breakfast together was."

"Me either," I say, because hers is the kind of comment you have to give a nothing answer to fast before someone says something like, "How could we eat together if Dad's never home?"

"How could we eat together? Dad's never home," Karen says.

The clock is ticking. I can tell they're all too tired to fight.

"I was home," Dad says, getting up, "and it's a good thing I was."

He kisses Karen on the forehead. "I'm glad you're okay." Karen looks at her plate and then grabs Dad around the waist to give him a quick squeeze and says, "Have a good day at work, Dad."

Dad ruffles my hair. "See ya."

He winks at Mom, and then he's gone. I should have asked him when he was coming home again.

"You kids can stay home from school if you want," Mom says. "You both had long nights."

Amanda comes up the back porch steps, waving before she opens the sliding glass door.

"Good morning," she says, and then to Karen, "Ready?"

"Just a second, I have to run upstairs."

"Karen, you should stay home today and rest." Mom's clearly not pleased.

"Why? Are you sick?" Amanda asks, taking a piece of toast off my plate and flicking my ear. I look at her throat as she swallows.

"No. I'm fine. Donnie's the sick one." Karen rushes out of the kitchen.

Amanda looks at Mom. Mom purses her lips and then says, "Donnie's fine, it's just an ear infection. Karen's the one that had to go to the hospital last night. For dehydration. You kids push yourselves too hard."

"IT WAS NOTHING!" Karen yells from upstairs.

Amanda looks at Mom for a long moment, about to say something. But Karen comes back into the kitchen with her backpack.

"Donnie, you were funny last night. I could hear you from my room telling Dad he was a prick. You should have a fever all the time, it makes you honest. Let's go, Amanda, we'll miss the bus. Two more months, then we'll have our licenses and can drive ourselves to school. That'll be the best," She manages to kiss Mom on the cheek and talk at the same time. "I'll buy lunch at school. Dad gave me money. Bye, Donnie. Feel better."

Amanda is still looking at Mom. She finally says, "Bye, Donnie," and follows Karen out through the sliding glass door.

"Well, you're not going to school," Mom says. "I'll make you a bed on the couch and you can watch TV."

15

"Donnie, why do you hang out with those guys?" Karen demands, her hands tight on the steering wheel. "They treat you like crap."

"Shut up," I say. I think they accidentally put some sort of jerk juice in her IV in the emergency room last week, because she's been a pain in my ass since she got home.

"Why should I shut up? It's true. Right, Mom?" Karen looks at Mom.

"Karen, don't look at me, look at the road. I think you should concentrate on driving and not on talking," Mom says, her hands spread on the dashboard in front of her. We come to a stoplight, and Mom says, "It certainly wasn't a very nice thing to do, Donnie, inviting you to the movies and then not showing up. What if Karen and I weren't out practicing? You'd be stuck out there in the cold for two hours! And you're just getting over an ear infection. I don't see why you didn't call us."

I slump down in the back seat. I wish Dad were here.

"It was just a joke," I mumble.

"Real funny joke," Karen says as the light turns green. She stomps on the gas, flattening Mom and me against our seats.

"Slow down!" Mom yells, both of her feet up on the dashboard. "Slow down!"

Karen takes her time slowing down, and says calmly, "Donnie, they made you stand out there like some sort of reject. Mom, I'm going to park at home and go over to Amanda's. You don't need that, Donnie."

"Karen, what about dinner? Slow down, please."

"I'll eat at Amanda's."

"Karen, it's eight o'clock. They eat at six. This is our street, slow down."

"I know this is our street! You think I don't know where we live? Amanda and I'll make something. Get off my back."

"You need to slow down when you're making a turn. And don't speak to me like that, Karen. I'm just concerned."

It's funny when you think about it, how you never know what's going to change Karen from a normal person into a screaming psycho. Karen pulls into our driveway and slams on the breaks.

"I made a mistake, Mom! One fucking mistake and you won't let me forget about it!"

"Karen," Mom says quietly, "watch your language."

Karen ignores her and opens the car door. Before she gets out, she says, "It's not like I did it on purpose, you know! It's not like I said, 'Know what would be fun? If I stopped eating and passed out in front of Mom and Dad so they could take me to the ER and treat me like a fucking half-wit for the rest of my life.' For fuck's sake, I'm eating! I eat all damn day long! I'm going to be a fat fuck, and then you'll be happy, right?"

She gets out of the car.

"Yes, Karen," Mom says, "I'll be happy when you're a fat . . . fuck."

Karen makes a noise that sounds like a laugh and stares at Mom from outside the car.

"I know your father and I didn't teach you to talk like that," Mom says.

"Yeah, well, you and your husband aren't the only people I learn things from. You don't get to decide what I know and what I don't." Karen slams the car door shut, leaving Mom and me in the car.

16

Mom calls over to Amanda's as soon as we get inside.

"Hi, Amanda, it's Karen's mom. Is she there?"

Mom opens the drawer by the phone and pulls out a stack of menus from restaurants that deliver. "Donnie, pick something out."

I lean against the counter and flip through the menus, stopping to watch Mom on the phone as she says, "Amanda, I don't care if she doesn't want to talk to me. Put her on the phone." It's weird to hear her use her mom voice on someone who's not her own kid. The mom voice works.

"Karen, I want you home. Now." Mom listens to Karen respond, and says, "Actually, Karen, I *am* the boss of you. Yes, really. Karen! If you think I am going to let you talk to me the way you did in the car tonight, you are sadly mistaken. Get home. Now."

. . .

Mom makes me go upstairs when we see Karen stomping across the back porch toward the sliding glass door. I head for Karen's room to look for the photos from the lake. She used to just keep them piled on her desk, but she hid them last week after she caught me flipping through them. She'd dragged me out of her room by my shirt and slammed the door in my face. I'm in most of those pictures, and the ones I'm not in are ones where I was taking the picture. She has no right to keep them from me, like it was just her summer and not mine. I've checked under her mattress already, but I realize now that I never checked the mattress of the rollaway bed that slides under her bed. I can hear Mom and Karen start in on each other downstairs, and I pull out the rollaway bed. I slide my hand under its mattress and rip open my palm on a bedspring. I press my hand against my shirt to stop it from bleeding all over the rug, and reach in with my other hand, avoiding the spring. I pull out a spiral notebook. Ha! Her journal. Even better than pictures. I open it up, ready to read every secret she'd ever wanted to keep from me, everything she and Amanda would stop talking about when I walked into the room. The notebook is set up like a regular journal, with a date on every page, but instead of secrets there are lists of foods for every day since we came home from the lake. As the dates get more recent, the lists get shorter and shorter.

I hear Mom and Karen laughing downstairs. I bet

they're hugging now. I put the notebook back under the mattress, and shove the rollaway bed back into place. When I get down to the kitchen, Karen eyes the Band-Aid on my palm for a second and then says, "Donnie, sorry I was such an A-hole in the car."

I shrug. "It's all right."

Mom and I order Chinese food, but Karen says she had it for lunch so she makes herself a can of soup.

"Karen." I'm surprised by the harshness of my whisper. I don't want to wake up Mom.

"Karen!"

"What? Is it your hand?" she sits up in bed and puts a hand in front of her face to block the hall light. I step into her room and shut the door. We're in the dark.

"I found your book tonight."

"I know. You bled on it. Why do you think I asked about your hand?"

"What is it? What's that book?"

I hear her lie back down in bed.

"It's for home economics. It's not what you think. We only have to keep track of certain foods, not everything we eat. We have to keep it all year and turn it in at the end. It's a quarter of our grade."

"Oh," I say, and I think, *Believe her believe her believe her.*

"Don't go through my stuff anymore, okay, Donnie?"

"Okay."

I'm about to walk out of her room when she says, "Mom's making me go to a counselor because she thinks there's something wrong with me. There's nothing wrong with me, Donnie. You know that, right?"

"Sure. I know that."

17

Mom calls Dad back as soon as I'm off the phone with him. He didn't ask to talk to her. He's taking me to the indoor stock-car races tomorrow. He said he might come by for dinner afterward. I report this to Mom, who is staring at the phone, like she can't believe he didn't want to talk to her. She squints her eyes and says, "What?"

"Don't yell at me. I'm just telling you what he said."

"I didn't yell at you." She has a point, but I think she's pissed off enough to yell, and I don't want her to do it at me since I didn't do anything but answer the phone.

I shrug. She looks at me for a long moment and says, "So this is the way it is." I know what she means. He hasn't come home since the trip to the ER. Mom calls him back and doesn't even say hello, she just snaps, "What?"

She listens, opens her mouth, and I think she's going to let him have it. Then she looks at me and says into the phone, "We'll talk about it tomorrow night . . . okay . . . see you then."

Then she claps her hands once and says, "So what should we make for Dad tomorrow night?"

I have no idea why she's asking me until I see her eyes are glassy and she has this huge fake plastic smile on her face, and I realize this is what she looks like when she's trying not to fall apart. I say, "I don't know. Spaghetti?"

She claps her hands again. "Yes! Spaghetti!"

Karen comes into the kitchen. "Don't make spaghetti for me. I'm eating at Amanda's."

Mom is opening cabinets and making a grocery list. "Karen, we're talking about tomorrow night. Tonight we're having chicken."

"I ate already. I'm going over to Amanda's."

Mom sighs. "You didn't eat already. You can see Amanda after your dinner. Set the table, please."

Dad picked me up this morning. He just beeped the horn in the driveway, didn't come in. He did wink and wave at Mom and Karen, who were standing in the doorway. I guess that's something. Mom will take Karen to counseling today, her first appointment. I'm not supposed to know.

Here's a secret: Dad sometimes talks to me about when he was little. It's a secret because everyone acts like Dad didn't even have a childhood. It's so weird, the family rules that you learn without ever being taught. Asking Dad about when he was a kid is against the rules. Ask him about it, and he'll stand up and walk out of the room. Or if you're in the car, he'll just turn on the radio and act like you're not even there. Ask Mom about it, and she'll say it's not your business and it's no big deal, there's no big story to tell. Ask Karen about it, and she'll either snap "I don't care" or we'll compare information and try to put Dad's past together, like a puzzle. The other rule is that even though we're not allowed to ask Dad about his childhood, he can sometimes bust out with a story from when he was a little kid. When this happens, you have to sit quietly and not ask questions, or he'll clam up and not say any more. I don't tell Karen everything he tells me, I keep some of it for myself.

Five minutes into the ride to the races, I wish I hadn't come. It's like being in a car with a stranger. He's wearing a winter coat I don't recognize, his hair is different, and his face looks kind of fat.

"Your mother says you're not friends with Chris and Benjamin anymore."

Way to get right to the point, asshole.

I'm almost yelling, "I'm still friends with them! Did Mom tell you that? That I'm not friends with them anymore?"

Dad calmly shakes his head. "I must have misunderstood. She just said you never got together with them after school or on weekends anymore. She told me about that night at the movies."

"So?" I say. "We still sit together at lunch."

"Oh. Well, then."

I hate that the few times Mom talks to him, she talks about me. I hate that she thinks she has any idea what's going on in my life and that she passes her bullshit theories on to Dad. He has no idea what's going on in my life. That's fine by me. I don't know him now. I debate telling him Mom told me not to talk to strangers. But I shrug instead, hoping he'll shut up about this.

"What happened, son, you just don't get along with them anymore?"

Way to completely miss the point, asshole.

"I told you, we're still friends. We just don't hang out as much," I say, and realize it's a lie. Chris and Bean barely acknowledge my existence anymore. The lunch table we share is divided in half. They're at one end and I'm at the other. They haven't talked to me in weeks. Apart from Mom and Karen, no one's really talked to me in weeks.

Dad nods. "School is hard."

I laugh. I can't help it. What a stupid thing to say.

"Dad, you are a true master of the obvious."

It's fascinating. You can actually see the blood rush up his neck and into his face. I bet he's counting to ten so he doesn't push me out of the car.

"When I was a kid, we'd say 'No shit, Sherlock.'" The red goes out of his face.

"Like Sherlock Holmes, right?"

He nods and says again quietly, "No shit, Sherlock."

We don't talk for a long while. When we pass a rusting VW bus with surfboards strapped to the top, Dad says, "Wow, they must be really, really lost." I say, "Let's make a sign that says, 'Landlocked state, asshole' and wave it at them."

Dad smiles. I watch the VW get smaller and smaller behind us in the side-view mirror, a cloud of black fumes disappearing behind it. I could be a surfer. Cousin Bobby surfed when he was out in California. His band was on tour and all of their L.A. shows got canceled. They met these surfers that let the band stay at their house and taught them all how to surf. We got a picture in the mail of Bobby on the beach. Karen laughed when she saw it. It did look kind of funny. Made up, almost. Bobby on the beach, looking out at the ocean, a hand shielding his eyes from the setting sun, like he was scoping out the waves. He was tan, healthy looking. Karen snorted and said, "When did Bobby get muscles?" His hair was wild, the way hair gets when you swim and then let the sun dry it. It'd be salty if he put it in his mouth.

After graduation I could leave for California. No, Hawaii. Right after the ceremony. I'd be in my gown, and underneath I'd be wearing surf shorts. No one would have any idea. The ceremony would end, I'd hug Karen and Mom and shake Dad's hand. Everyone would be throwing their caps into the air, hugging each other, crying, and ignoring me. Then this ancient VW bus would rumble up, beep, and the side door would open and I'd jump in. And I'd be gone. Everyone would stop what they were doing and watch us drive away. I'd never satisfy their curiosity. I'd never talk to any of them again.

"Your grandmother was tall."

I'm not in the VW anymore. I'm not peeling off my graduation gown. I'm in a car with Dad and he's just said something.

"What?"

He looks at me nervously and swallows.

"I said your grandmother, my mother, was tall."

One night last winter Karen and I were out behind the house kicking at the snow, waiting for Mom and Dad to finish fighting. I was bending over, packing a snowball to throw at Karen, and I felt her fingers on my wrist. At first I thought she was going to try to pin my arm behind my back and push my face in the snow, and then try to sit on me, but then I looked up and saw a deer in the dark by the shed. Karen barely shook her head, telling me not to move. We looked at the deer, the deer looked at us. We all three breathed white breath out of our noses. I knew I wasn't supposed to move, wasn't supposed to speak, or it would run away.

It's the same thing with Dad when he decides to open up. If you make any sudden moves, he'll bolt, or at least get real quiet and ignore you. I'm supposed to be touched that he's opening up. It's supposed to be a "special moment." I'm sup- posed to sit here and ask gentle questions about when he was a kid, and maybe he'll poop out a tiny turd of information and I'm supposed to think it's a diamond. Forget it. I'm not playing. I don't care if he's looking at me like a kicked puppy, waiting for me to ask . . .

"How tall was she?"

If I could suck the words back into my mouth, I would. It's just so hard, he sits there looking wounded, like every second I don't say something is tearing his heart out of his chest.

Dad exhales and smiles.

"She was six feet, one inch. Her mother was taller: six three."

"Wow," I say. I mean it. It's something I didn't know. I've seen one picture of them, and that was just of their heads. They both looked old. I picture long bodies reaching out from where the picture cut off.

He nods.

A nod. That counts as him saying something, meaning now it's my turn. Sneaky bastard.

Fine, he wants to play that way . . .

"Really?" I ask.

He looks at me, brows creased. He's on to me. He nods again. I've got it.

"Did they play basketball?"

He smiles. "Yes. Both played in high school."

I wait for him to say more. He looks at me, waiting for another question that he'll either answer or ignore. I can't play this game for very long anymore. It pisses me off too much. I used to think it was fun, figuring out exactly what to say to him so that he'd answer back with actual information. I thought it was like being a spy. I'd report back to Karen what I'd learned. Then we'd put it together with what we already knew and try to tell each other the story of when he was a little kid. It was always full of holes. I can't believe he expects me to sit here and spoon-feed his attempts at opening up.

"Did your dad play basketball?"

He looks at me. I think, *Not the question you expected was it, asshole?* I broke the rule, the talk-only-about-people-that-Dad-mentions-first rule. I'm tired of tiptoeing.

"Did he? Did my grandfather play basketball?"

"I wouldn't know," he says, and then looks at the road. This answer is supposed to shut me up. I'm supposed to give him a long look and then stare out the window and not talk for two hours.

"Why wouldn't you know?"

I swear I can hear Dad telling himself not to punch me: *Don't do it, don't do it, don't do it.*

"That's the sort of thing," he finally answers, "that boys who grew up with their Dads would know."

"No shit, Sherlock."

Note to self: Learn difference between thinking of brilliant things to say and actually saying them.

Dad's gone cold next to me.

"Dad?"

He shakes his head.

"You're wrong, you know," I say. "Growing up with your dad doesn't mean you know jack shit about him."

We'd go to California first. Kind of inevitable on the way to Hawaii. I'd be a quick learner, the quickest anyone ever saw. I'd work for a couple months at an open-air taco place on the beach that all the locals go to, till I was ready to move on. Then I'd be gone again.

I'd go down to the docks and make a deal with some rich guy to take me with him to Hawaii in exchange for working on his yacht. He'd have a daughter. Hot.

My first day in Hawaii I wouldn't have anywhere to go, so I'd hitchhike from the docks and get dropped off at the first beach I see. I'd ditch my stuff under a palm tree, grab my board, and head straight for the waves. I wouldn't know it, but it'd be a locals beach, and as I paddled out, the locals would move together in the water and plan how to beat the crap out of me. They'd watch me catch my first wave and ride it all the way into the beach. I'd get out of the water, feeling all of their eyes on my back. I'd jam my board in the sand and hold my hand up above my eyes to block the sun and watch the locals in the water. I'd hear a voice next to me, turn, and see the local legend they call Dingo standing next to me. I'd think he was going to beat the snot out of me, but instead he'd say, "You're raw, but you've got talent."

He'd offer to train me and tell me I can crash with him in the house where all the local surfers live. The house would be this sort of ramshackle sprawl on a bluff over the ocean, so you could see how big the waves were from the porch, which is where Dingo would cook on the grill for the whole house. There'd be a lot of people living in the house, so you would just have to find a place to sleep wherever. At first I'd crash out on the couch in the living room, then Kula, this really hot girl, would tell me I could room with her. We'd spend a lot of time making out, facing each other on my surfboard in the water.

18

This is what I feel like: I'm trying to keep my balance in a cold, hard wind, standing on the tip of a gigantic metal cone that towers over everything in my world. I have this feeling that if I can stay balanced, things will stay the same, as bad as they are. They won't get any worse. But if I lose my balance, I'll go flying off the tip of the cone, and the whole world will come apart. I have a list in my head of things I have to do to keep the balance.

1. I have to talk to at least three people at school every day. Chris and Bean don't even say "Hey" to me anymore. Every time I talk to someone, it's like an invisible octopus tentacle shoots out of me and attaches itself to them. So no matter how hard they try to beat me back until I disappear, I'm

still here because I've got these tentacles attached to them and they keep me from floating away.

2. I have to watch Karen eat at least what Mom puts on her plate every night. Because if she eats, then maybe she's not sick, and that one trip to the emergency room can be just that—something that happened just that one time. She's in counseling, and she wouldn't be in counseling unless it was making her better, right?

3. I have to see Dad at least once every ten days, because if I can get him to come by every ten days, it means that he's just a busy guy, and that we're basically a normal family.

4. I have to make sure Amanda sleeps over at least once each weekend. This means that if it's Saturday night and she's not at our house, I say to Karen, "Where's Amanda?" They're not spending as much time together anymore, and I think Mom's worried about it too, because when I ask, "Where's Amanda?" Mom gets Karen to call and invite her to sleep over. Karen's having a best friend means that she's okay, and Amanda wouldn't sleep over at our house if we weren't normal, so of course if she sleeps over, it means we're all right.

Today was a good day at school. Mr. Delancey had us do a group science project in experimental bio where we tested how flammable candy is. That means that before first period was even over, I'd talked to the four people in my group. That means that I talked to one more person than I needed to, and if only two people talk to me tomorrow, it's all right, because I'll just use that extra one from today to make up for it.

Karen and Amanda are sitting on the front steps scrunched together under a blanket when I get home. It's freezing out, and they have on hats and scarves and gloves, and they've got the blanket pulled up under their chins. They're both laughing but have tears on their faces, which usually means they were fighting and then made up. They don't move when I try to walk past them up the steps. Amanda says, "Hey, Donnie, I have to tell you something."

Today I'm going to count Amanda as the fifth person I've talked to today. Usually I just count her as family, which doesn't really count, but since I haven't talked to five people in one day in over four weeks, I'm letting her in.

"What?" I say, and I don't let myself hope that she's forgiven me for the whole lying-about-sleeping-with-her thing and that she wants us to be friends again and by the way do I want to go make out with her in the woods behind the baseball field?

"My dad's moving us back to Chicago."

Karen starts crying, and there is no more balance, and I think, *This is what falling feels like.*

19

The night when they took Karen to the hospital and I got in a fight with the clock seems like it was forever ago. Amanda's been in Chicago for a week already. My family seems like we are plowing through time, trying to get our distance from what happened, even if we never talk about that night or the fact that Karen's in counseling or that Dad never comes home or that I'm flunking three subjects and am home every day after school and all weekend. No one at school knew what happened, and even though I opened my mouth the next day at lunch to tell the story, Chris looked at me and said, "Shut up." It's amazing, the way him saying that made my mouth clamp shut, like it was connected to a remote control in his hand.

Karen and Mom have been fighting and making up

every other day. One day they're screaming at each other, and the next Karen's practically in Mom's lap while she makes tiny braids in Karen's hair. It's like there's a hiccup in the way time works, and they can only live the same two days over and over again.

It's been different the past couple days, though, the way Mom's been watching Karen. It's because when Amanda was over last week, and Mom asked if they were going to eat dinner, Karen said, "I ate at Amanda's already." And Amanda looked right at Mom and said, "No, you didn't." Karen made some excuse and dragged Amanda out of the kitchen.

Mom and Karen have been circling each other all night. I think, *Tigers. Grrr.* Mom watches Karen closely, and Karen pretends not to notice. I watch them both and wait for something to happen. I think Mom is having some sort of out-of-body experience. She walks around like she doesn't recognize our house or her family, and what she does see puts dark shadows on her face.

"Mom, come on. Just check it off." This is humiliating. My math teacher found out I forged my math midterm progress report, which said that I'm failing, which I am, and now Mom checks my math homework every night.

"Hold on. You didn't finish this one," she says, tapping her pen on the last problem.

"That's the extra credit. You get credit just for trying," I say. It's a lie. It's not extra credit, it's just a problem that sucks.

She falls for it, sort of. She signs the page and says, "Finish the extra credit, okay?"

I wait till she's back to watching Karen across the table before I say, "Fine." Then she glances at me like she's surprised I'm standing there.

"Karen," she says, "do you want some ice cream?"

Karen shakes her head and finishes drawing a straight line across the graph she's working on.

"I'll have ice cream," I say, still standing next to Mom. I'm too mad to leave like she wants me to.

"Your brother's having ice cream," Mom says, not looking at me.

"So?" Karen says.

"Maybe some fruit?" Mom asks. I can tell this is leading nowhere good. I sit down at the table.

Karen looks up from her graph.

"Mom, what are you doing? You're just sitting there. Don't you have something to do?"

It *is* kind of weird. Mom's just sitting at the kitchen table in her robe and wet hair from her nightly shower, watching Karen. I know Karen can feel it, even if she's looking at her homework. What I don't understand is why Karen doesn't say anything, why she doesn't scream, "Stop staring at me!"

"Mom, why are you staring at Karen?" I ask, still mad about the homework.

Both Karen and Mom whip their heads around to look at me. They exchange a look, and Karen gives Mom a small, pleading shake of her head and I think, *Oh shit, what did I do?* I pressed the bad button, the one that makes terrible things happen. You can't unexplode a bomb.

Mom sighs and reaches into her robe pocket and brings out a folded pamphlet.

"I just think," she says to Karen, "that maybe you should . . ." She pushes the pamphlet across the table.

"What?" Karen says, knocking it to the floor. I can see it says Kennedy Inpatient Treatment Center. "What do you think I should do, Mom, what?"

"You know what, Karen. I've been watching you . . ."

"Oh, really, I haven't noticed."

"And I just think that it would help. So does your counselor. They do good work, it's a good place, Karen."

"You talked to Marie about this? You planned this with her? She's *my* counselor, Mom! You have no right to talk to her! I'm not going, Mom." Karen's face has gone white and still. "There's nothing wrong with me."

"Then prove me wrong. Go there and they'll send you right back with a note pinned to your shirt that says, 'There's nothing wrong with this one.'"

"I'm not going."

"Karen, I've called your school. They know you'll be out for two weeks. Your dad and I are going to drive you to the . . . place, tomorrow."

"You told Dad?" Karen yells. "Why did you tell him? I'm not going anywhere with him!"

"What's wrong with Karen?" I ask, feeling sick.

"Nothing," Karen says. "Mom's just being an asshole."

I whisper, "Whoa," and get up from the table. It's too big, what's happening. There's no room for me.

From my room I hear the rest of the fight. What's weird is that even though they're both trying to yell, it gets caught in their throats. So it comes out with no force. Here's the argument:

Karen: What, were you just not going to tell me? Were you just going to throw me in the trunk and hope I didn't asphyxiate on the way there? You're so stupid, Mom. You think I didn't know you were planning this. I found the pamphlet in your room. I knew what you were doing. You don't have anything better to do than watch me eat. Even Marie says you have no life outside of Donnie and me. I feel sorry for you. I'm embarrassed for you because there's nothing wrong with me and you're just a bored housewife inventing things that are wrong with your kids because you have nothing better to do. Why does Dad have to come? I don't want him to come! Who else knows? I'd better be back for Christmas, because you said Amanda could come and visit. You're jealous I have a best friend and all you have is Aunt Jannie and she never even visits anymore. Why are you doing this to me? Who else did you tell? What are you going to tell Donnie? Don't tell him anything, I don't want him to know anything. I bet you hope he gets another ear infection because you love it when he's sick because then you get to act like a real mom. Why don't you just pop some more pills into him, he can't get more screwed up than he already is. This is seriously messed up, Mom, I can't believe you're doing this to me. It's not going to change anything because I'm fine, there's nothing wrong with me and I hate you and I won't forgive you for this, ever.

Mom: Of course I was going to tell you! I just couldn't find the right time. Don't be ridiculous, I would never lock you in a trunk. I don't see how I'm an idiot when you're the one who thinks I won't notice that as soon as I turn my head, your dinner magically disappears from your plate. Funny how I always find it in your trash can later. You didn't think I knew about that, did you? You are in way over your head, young lady. You have taken this entirely too far and you can be as nasty as you want to be to me but it won't change the fact that tomorrow morning you are getting in that car with your father and me. He's your father, that's why he has to come. You'll be there as long as you need to be and if you want to be home in time to see Amanda at Christmas, then it's up to you to get yourself well. This isn't about Donnie. This is about you. You can hate me all you want to, Karen, but you are going to get yourself out of whatever phase it is that you're in. I want you well. I just want you well again.

"Donnie, I'm leaving." I know she's leaving. I've been up since really early this morning, waiting to see if she would say goodbye before she left. I open my bedroom door. She's been crying and she's wearing her jacket.

"I hate them," she says.

I don't know how to answer so I say, "I know."

"Go out on the steps if they start in on each other. I left you candy in the tin."

"Thanks," I say.

"You can't call me up there. But call Amanda in Chicago if . . . if it gets bad here, all right?"

I nod. She gives me a quick, fierce hug. I didn't realize she'd gotten so small. I pull back and look at her, my hands on her sides.

"Shut up," she says, and walks down the stairs.

20

I'm becoming invisible. Every day more and more light shines through me. I think about writing Karen at the hospital and telling her. If I wrote her and told her I was becoming invisible, I think she'd tell me to stop being so dramatic, and she'd say that she understood.

Once I realized that I was becoming invisible, once I realized that no one really noticed me anymore, I stopped fighting it. I stopped taking the tiny bit of room they left me on the bench at the lunch table and sat by myself at the end of the teacher's table, which is pretty much the worst place any kid can sit, ever. Unless that kid's invisible, and then it doesn't matter. Every day since Karen's been gone, I practice floating through the school halls like a ghost. I don't touch anyone and I imagine that the times I do brush up against their arms it feels like a clammy, cold breath on their skin. I sit in the back of class and I don't raise my hand. I ignore everyone, even the teachers. Not the kind of ignoring where you jut out your chin and hope that everyone notices you ignoring them. I ignore them like we're not even in the same universe. I ignore them because it's easy: I'm not even here. My goal is to get through the whole school day without anyone talking to me. I decide once I do that, I'll become a superhero. I'll become Donnie Disappeared.

21

Mom and Karen are still at the table in the kitchen. An hour ago I could tell by the way Karen kept rearranging the rice on her plate that they'd end up sitting like this, Mom's plate empty and Karen's heavy with cold food. When she first got back from the hospital, I felt like I was part of a football team made up of all the people set on keeping her well. Her nutritionist. Her doctor. Her therapist. Mom. Dad. And me—the one that no one had asked to join the team, but who kept showing up to practice. I pictured us all in team jerseys standing firmly with arms crossed in front of us, daring Karen's sickness to try to get past. I thought we'd be strong enough.

I've put all the dishes in the dishwasher except for Karen's, which I left in front of her. I washed all the pots and wiped down the counters and the table, working around

Karen's plate and glass and napkin. I clean as long as I can, not wanting to leave, wanting to see if Mom will find a way to get her to eat. Finally, when I start to empty the crumbs out of the toaster, Mom says, "Donnie, please go do your homework."

I leave because if I argue, it might give Karen a chance to escape upstairs and lock herself in her room. Keeping the attention on her is really important. I go to the den, where I can look over the back of the couch and listen to them and watch their reflections against the dark outside in the sliding glass door.

Neither one of them says anything for a long time. And then Mom says, "Oh, Karen." And I can hear she's crying.

"Mom." Karen's annoyed voice.

"It just hurts me, Karen, to see you like this."

"So don't look at me, then. Leave me alone."

"You know I can't do that. You're my daughter, it hurts me so much, watching you do this to yourself."

"So don't watch."

"Do you want to hurt your family, is that what it is? You want to make us suffer right along with you?"

"For Christ's sake, Mom, not everything is about you."

"Just tell me what I can do, tell me how to make you better, and I'll do it."

"You can't."

"Your brother is terrified. You see the way he watches you? If you're not home after school, he asks me if you've gone back, if we had to take you back to that place."

That's true, I do ask that.

Karen doesn't have an answer for that.

"He loves you so much, Karen. We all love you so much, but this is tearing us apart. I need you to help us help you, tell us how to help you. Just eat ten bites, eat ten bites so your poor mother can get some sleep tonight."

Karen snorts at the "poor mother" part. I agree, it's a little over the top.

"Please, Karen, ten bites. For Donnie."

There's a pause, a small sound of a fork against a plate.

"Good girl. That's a girl."

22

Karen's spinning me around, wrapping the scarf all the way up my neck and over my face. It's the day after Christmas, which means it's time for Karen to dress me up in every piece of clothing we got for presents. I'm already wearing jeans, pajamas, four shirts, and the ugly orange anorak Aunt Janice sent. It actually wasn't a bad Christmas. Dad came home Christmas eve, and there haven't been any big fights. I think everyone needed to be okay, at least for a few days. Karen's working on pulling a hat down over my scarf-covered head when Mom comes stomping into the den with Dad.

"Karen!" I can see through the knit of the scarf that Mom's got her hands on her hips. Bad sign. "I just got a call from Amanda's dad. He wanted to make sure we knew what time to pick Amanda up at the airport tomorrow."

My mouth drops open. Dad and I both look at Karen. She laughs because I'm still wrapped up in the scarf, and then looks at Mom and Dad, annoyed. I pull the scarf off my face.

"What? I told you that," she snaps.

"No you did not, young lady. You most certainly did not. You told us she couldn't come to visit, that she wanted to be in Chicago for New Year's."

"Sorry." Karen couldn't be more bored with the conversation. "Amanda's coming to visit. She needs us to pick her up tomorrow."

Mom and Dad stare at her; the holler is building up inside them. Karen cuts them off with a curt, "Shut up."

They don't. In fact, they open up with all their words and their volume, and Karen answers back with hers. I rise above the noise, rise right out of the den and up to my room. She's coming to visit, and things will be like they were before.

We're in the living room. Mom's decided this is where we should sit to catch up with Amanda. I sit between Mom and Dad on the couch. Amanda and Karen sit in armchairs, not looking at each other. Mom made us all giant Santa Claus mugs of hot chocolate "Just like you girls like it." Amanda sips at hers, and Karen just leaves hers on the end table. Mom's keeping up appearances, except she forgets what our appearance was. Amanda gave me a hug when she came in. I can't even act disinterested. I can't not look at her. I want to pull words out of her mouth; I want to hear her say something, because even though she's talking, she's not saying anything at all.

"How's your dad, Amanda?" Mom asks.

"He's fine. He's the contractor for a new mini-mall, so . . ."

"Oh, that's good."

"Does he still have the truck?" Dad asks.

"Um, actually, I drive it now." Her eyes flick over to Karen, who couldn't be less impressed. "He bought himself a sedan." Dad loses interest and looks out the window at the Christmas lights on our bushes.

I can't wait till Amanda and Karen go to bed. Because then, when Karen goes to brush her teeth, she'll leave her bedroom door open and I'll stick my head in and talk to Amanda. She'll ask how Karen is and I'll tell her. Then maybe she'll ask about me and I'll tell her the truth. I'll tell her that I'm about to disappear. Then maybe we'll make out.

Mom runs out of questions, and sends us all upstairs with, "Well, you must be tired. We made up the spare bed in Karen's room for you."

"Hi," I say, sticking my head into Karen's room. Amanda is sitting on the rollaway bed, a yearbook open on her lap.

"Hi," she says. "How are things?"

"All right. What's Chicago like?"

"It's all right. The school's, like, four times the size of this one."

"Are you on the soccer team?"

"Not this year," she says quietly, looking back at the yearbook.

"Oh." I can't think of anything else to say. Nothing happens the way it should.

"Well," I say, "see you tomorrow."

"Okay. See you tomorrow." I take a step, and stop when she says, "Donnie."

Ask me to make out, ask me to make out, ask me to make out. I step back through the door.

"Last summer was fun, wasn't it?"

"Yeah," I say. "It was the best."

She grins at me, a real, wide smile. Karen's out of the bathroom.

"Donnie, what are you doing?"

"Nothing," I say, and walk out of her room.

Amanda calls, "Good night!" after me.

It's so quiet in Karen's room. I can't believe they've fallen asleep. When I came back from the bathroom, I stood outside Karen's door and heard them say low good-nights to each other. I watched as the sliver of light under their door disappeared, and stood there listening to them not say anything for a long, long time. Nothing is the way it was. They should be up for hours, laughing, screeching, rearranging Karen's furniture, dyeing their hair, and going downstairs to make snacks. Instead there's just silence.

I get into bed and debate kicking the wall really hard to

wake them up, but fall asleep instead. I wake up, barely hearing Amanda say, "I did it," through the wall.

I press the water glass I brought upstairs with me against the wall, and put my ear against it.

"What?" Karen asks, sounding wide awake. I can hear them perfectly through the glass.

"Rio slipped me the hot beef injection." She and Karen explode into laughter. "No way," I whisper.

"No way!" Karen gasps. "Really?" She sounds equally surprised and impressed.

"Yep."

"How . . . I don't know . . . How was it?"

"It was . . . weird. Good."

They laugh at that. I can hear the creak of their beds, and guess that they've turned over on their sides to face each other. I picture them trying to make out each other's faces through the darkness in the room. I hate them both.

"He said he'd wait as long as I wanted. And then . . . I didn't want to wait anymore."

"Does your dad know?"

"Apparently," Amanda says. "He actually keeps track of the condoms in his drawer."

"No way! What'd he do?"

"He called Rio and told him if he got me pregnant, he'd kill him."

Karen snorts. "Your dad's so macho."

"I know. It drives me insane."

I take the glass away from the wall and flop back on my bed. I can feel every drop of blood pushing through my veins. I can hear my heartbeat in my ears and there's a hollow-feeling space in my head. I put the glass back up to the wall.

". . . Dad wouldn't even look at me for three days. So I finally wrote him a letter and taped it to his dashboard."

"Really? What did it say?" Why did Karen have to sound so excited?

"Well . . ." There's a sound of shuffling paper and then laughter.

"You brought it with you?" Karen's obviously impressed.

"I don't know, it worked so well for me, I thought maybe you could use it."

More laughter. I make a plan to sneak into the room tomorrow and find the note.

"Dear Dad."

"Ooh, good start. I'll use that." Karen giggles.

I take the glass away from the wall for a second to give my ear a rest and wait for them to stop laughing.

"Okay . . . 'Dear Dad, It's been three days since I told you about Rio and me, and you still haven't looked me in the eye. I know you think I'm your little girl, but I'm not. I'm my own woman, my own person—'"

"Oooh, that's good," Karen whispers, and then rushes out with a laugh. "Okay, okay, keep going."

"Thanks. Okay, so . . . 'I'm my own woman, my own

person, and you don't own me or my sexuality. Me having sex wasn't an act against you, it was something I did for me. It has nothing to do with you. If you really loved me, you wouldn't treat me like I disgust you. My virginity was not yours to protect, it was mine. My body, my life, my choices. If you can't love me now because I'm not "pure," then that's your problem, and I hope you get over it. Love, Panda.'"

"Holy shit, you gave that to him?" I can hear Karen sit up in bed. "Amanda, that's incredible. That really worked?"

"No, it sort of pissed him off more. He's not ready to admit he doesn't own me, body and mind. At least he looked me in the eyes to yell at me, though. We're talking again, but it's weird. Something's totally changed."

There's a silence as we all think about this. I picture Amanda and her father in their Chicago kitchen eating pancakes and not looking at each other.

"I wish you still lived here," Karen says. "You could have talked to Mom about it."

There's a long pause.

"Actually, I did."

"You talked to Mom? When?" There's ice in Karen's voice.

"A couple weeks ago." Amanda heard the chill too. She's measuring out her words. "I called and she said you weren't home. I could tell you were, though. She said I sounded upset and she asked me what was wrong, so I told her. She was really cool about it."

Karen doesn't answer. After a long while Amanda says, "What about you? Are you seeing anybody?"

I know that things are bad between them, for Amanda to have to ask that. They're strangers now.

"No, I'm not." Karen's words clack together, falling out of her mouth. "You know. I was out of school, and then it was weird when I went back. I couldn't even get my driver's license because I was out so much."

There's another long pause and Amanda asks, "What was it like in that place? I mean, we've never really talked about what it was . . ." Amanda trails off and then says, "Sorry. Never mind. I didn't mean to pry."

"No, it's fine," Karen says. "No one here asks about it. Not that I'd answer if they did. It was weird, Amanda. All these girls, all of them screwed up the same way I am. You know how we used to read those disease-of-the-week books?"

"The ones like about drug abuse and that girl that got pregnant by her dad?"

"Yeah, those. And remember the one about the girl who would only eat lettuce leaves and licorice?"

"You must be referring to the classic, *Dying to Be Thin*."

They both laugh.

"Yeah. That one."

Silence.

"Well, what about it?"

"Oh. Well, I don't know. I thought it would be like that."

"Like that how?"

"Well, you know how at the end of the book, after Elsie's roommate dies of a heart attack, and that night all of her friends on the ward break into the kitchen and eat ice cream to honor her because it was her favorite food before she got sick?"

Amanda laughs. "Okay, you obviously remember that book much better than I do."

"We had a copy on the ward and we used to act it out at night between bed checks," Karen says matter-of-factly.

Amanda says, "Oh."

I close my eyes and press my ear harder against the glass.

"Anyway," Karen continues, "in the book all the girls go to group the next day and Elsie has this huge epiphany. She decides she doesn't want to end up like her roommate, and for the first time when it comes her turn to speak, instead of passing she says, 'My name is Elsie, and my grandpa molested me when I was three. And that is why I do this to myself.' And everyone else in group claps, and then one by one all of her friends stand up and say things like, 'My name is Sarah, my parents got divorced, and that is why I do this to myself.' Or 'My name is Candy, and I was a really fat kid, and that's why I do this to myself," and everyone ends up crying and hugging and the therapist does this victory fist into the air, and then the next chapter takes place two weeks later and Elsie is getting ready to check out, and as she's leaving, this new girl is on her way in, and Elsie looks deep into the new girl's eyes and says, 'You're gonna make it, sweetie. I promise.'"

What the fuck is she talking about?

After a second Amanda says, "I guess I remember some of that."

"Well, it wasn't like that at all," Karen grumbles.

"Well, no shit, Karen, that was a book." Amanda half-laughs, half-yells.

I nod. Yeah, no shit, Sherlock.

Karen laughs. "I know! I know it was just a book, but . . ."

There's a long silence. I wonder for a second if they know I'm listening and have started passing notes instead. But then Karen says, her voice sounding more tired than before, "There wasn't any one clear-cut reason why anyone was there. We all just had different pieces of each other's stories. Being in there, you find out there's nothing special about you. The doctors know everything that happened to you and every-thing that is going to happen to you. We all stopped getting our periods. Lots of girls were losing the hair on their heads but having it sprout out like down all over their bodies. We all had moments when it felt like our hearts were beating out the wrong rhythm. We all had weird pains all the time. And all of us were trying to figure out how to get out of there without getting better. The doctors try and convince us that we're not in control of it, and we try to remember that we are. There's nothing unique about it when you're in there. It's different out here. And what that stupid book doesn't talk about is that after you dig down to find out the things that make you this way, after you flick out the seed that everything grew from, there's still a hole there where the seed was. You still have to do something about the hole."

I wait for Amanda to say something. I bet she can't breathe either. I try to catch my breath, and think, *She'll get better, she'll get better, she'll get better.*

"I'll tell you something about it, though," Karen starts talking again, "that even the doctors there don't know. There was this sweater. Ages and ages ago some girl brought it to the ward, and it's been passed from girl to girl ever since. It's cable knit, one of those Irish fisherman sweaters. And it's small, almost a little-kid size. Since they tried to keep us from knowing how much we weighed, how small we were, we'd use the sweater. Only the very smallest person on the ward got to wear it. It was like a prize."

After a long moment I hear Amanda squeak out, "Karen, that's so scary. That makes me want to cry." That's a lie, I can tell she's already crying.

"Well, relax, because I never got to wear it. I got better instead," Karen says sharply.

I hear Amanda turn over. She'd be facing the wall now, facing me, just three feet away. I lie down on my bed and move the glass so I can be lying down and listening at the same time. I imagine her voice vibrating the glass against my fingers.

"Karen," she asks cautiously, "how come we don't talk anymore?"

Karen doesn't hesitate. "Because I know what you think about me."

"What?"

"You think I'm stupid. You think I let myself get tricked into this."

"I don't think that." Amanda's voice has shrunk; I have to strain to hear it.

"Yes, you do. You've never had to work a day in your life on your body, and that means that you will never understand."

"What are you talking about?" Amanda raises her voice. "Karen, I work out in the gym five days a week to keep in shape so I can get back on the soccer team. *That's* working on your body. Not what . . . what you do."

Karen answers back in a shrill falsetto, "Gosh, Amanda, I never realized that there was more than one way to get skinny! Maybe I should go out for the soccer team. Then I'll love every inch of my body, just like you!"

"Oh, so now you want me to lie here and list all the things I hate about myself? Is that what you would do in there with all your clever friends? Laugh at the doctors who are trying to help you, and hate yourself as much as possible? I'm not going to do that, Karen. I *like* my body, I like what it does for me—"

"Well, obviously Rio likes it too."

"Why are you doing this? God, what is wrong with you, Karen? Don't you remember . . ." Amanda sighs instead of finishing her sentence.

"What?"

"It's just that we knew about all this stuff. I mean, we'd talk about how fattist magazines were, and we'd get all excited when an actress that weighed more than eighty pounds starred in a movie. I mean, we'd talk about how messed up it was that the world made us think we needed to be that thin. I just don't see . . . I mean, don't you feel like . . ."

"Like what? A sell out? An idiot? A bad, bad feminist?"

"I wasn't going to say that."

"What then?"

"Just, how could you let it happen? Didn't you feel it was happening?"

I wake up with my back at a right angle to the wall that my head is resting against. For a second I think I'm paralyzed. Amanda is on the phone in Mom's room,

"I just want to come home early, that's all. . . . Rio! Just come pick me up at the airport, okay?"

I go down to the kitchen and sit at the table with Mom and Dad. Karen's leaning against the counter.

"I don't know, she's homesick. Maybe she wants to be with her boyfriend for New Year's eve. I don't know, she just wants to leave." Karen doesn't seem sad about it at all. Amanda walks into the kitchen.

"Well, we're sure sad to see you go so soon. It's been so long since we've seen you," Mom says, giving Amanda a hug. "We didn't even have time to talk."

Amanda gives a furtive look toward Karen.

"I just miss my boyfriend, and I have midterms."

All eyes are on Karen, who is still looking pleased, still leaning against the counter. They barely hug good-bye. Karen doesn't even go with Dad to bring Amanda to the airport. She just watches as he drives Amanda away. Karen looks satisfied. She gives me a sideways look.

"What are you going to do with yourself now, with no one for you to follow around all weekend?"

"I hate you," I say, and I do, because I don't know the answer to her question and I don't know what is wrong with my life and I don't know what to do to make it better.

23

Mom started taking a class in tax law when Karen got out of the hospital, so she can work as an accountant like she did before she had us. Karen says Mom never wanted to stop working, but Dad made her when we were born. My sister really wants me to hate our dad with her. She's always listing the crappy things he's done, and the way he's never apologized for any of it. What she doesn't know is that I keep my own list in my head, and for everything she says, I think of something from my own list. Like how when he would make chili, he'd tell Mom and Karen there were no girls allowed in the kitchen, and he'd stand me on a chair next to him and let me mix up the corn bread batter with my hands while he made the chili. Or how when I used to be scared of thunder, he would find me hiding under the front-hall table and get down on his hands and knees and crawl under the table and sit next to me until the storm was over.

When Mom told Dad on the phone that she was taking a class, I could tell he wasn't happy because she said, "Joseph, you don't have a say in this. You forfeited your say in our lives when you changed zip codes."

Mom's always tired when she comes home from class, and tonight she has a headache too, which means I'll be waiting till tomorrow to get her to sign the science test I flunked. I'm setting the table for dinner when Karen walks into the kitchen. She's been up in her room since I got home from school. She doesn't look well. She's got bags under her eyes, and she's got her arms folded and pressed against her stomach.

Mom doesn't notice her come in, and is bouncing pasta up and down in a strainer over the sink.

"Mom?" Karen says.

Mom keeps bouncing the pasta and doesn't look at Karen.

"Karen, my head is killing me. If you want to complain about dinner, do it to someone else. You can make your steamed veggies if you don't want pasta."

"Mom? I don't—"

"Damnit, Karen!" Mom slams the pasta strainer on the counter and spins around to face Karen.

"Mom, I don't feel well." Karen sits down at the kitchen table, still clutching her stomach.

"What doesn't feel well?" I can hear Mom try to soften her voice. It doesn't work.

"My insides," Karen groans, bending farther forward and looking up at Mom, and then me. I put down the plate I'm holding and sit in the chair next to Karen.

"Well, have you eaten today?" Mom snaps.

Karen nods.

"What did you have?" Mom's got her I'm-not-going-to-like-your-answer face on.

"Mom, I told you. I ate. I ate enough."

"Karen," Mom says in a pleading voice, "why should I believe you?"

"Because I'm telling the truth. These aren't hunger pains. I know what those feel like." There's pride in her voice. Mom ignores it.

"Do you feel like you're going to throw up?" she asks.

"No. My insides feel like they're twisted up in knots."

"Well . . ." Mom sighs. "What do you want to do?"

"I don't know!" It's the closest to whining I've ever heard Karen come.

"You know, you could have told me this earlier and we could have taken you to see Dr. Frasier! It's seven o'clock at night now!"

"I'm sorry, Mom. I just didn't want you to have to miss class and yell at me."

"Why would I yell at you?" Mom yells, then turns around, dumps the pasta into the sink, and turns on the garbage disposal. She leans over the sink, watching the pasta spin down the drain. I can see she's taking deep breaths, maybe even crying.

"Get your coat, Karen," she says, switching off the disposal. "Donnie—"

"I'm coming too," I say, standing up.

She nods and says, "We'll find a drive-through and get some burgers on the way to the ER."

Karen lies on a waiting-room couch with her head on Mom's lap and her knees curled against her stomach. She fell asleep almost as soon as we got here.

"Do you want more fries?" Mom whispers to me sitting next to her.

I shake my head.

"Are you okay?" she whispers.

I nod. It's a lie. I'm not okay. But Mom's not okay either, so what does it matter? I'm doing my part to make things better, or at least not make them worse.

"My quiet little boy," she whispers, putting her arm around me and pulling me close to her. "I wish you talked to me like you used to. You used to tell me the most wonderful stories. When things are better, when there's more time, I want you to tell me all of the stories you've been saving up in your head. I want to hear them all."

I nod. I could do that. I could talk to her again.

A woman and a swollen-looking girl with pasty skin and

a racking cough sit on the couch across from us. The young girl doesn't even look at us, she just curls up like Karen, with her head in the woman's lap. The woman, I guess it's her mom, rubs the girl's back, just like Mom is doing to Karen. We all sit there for a long time, not speaking. There's a TV in the corner and the long-haired security guard who was standing by the automatic doors walks over and switches it on, with the volume turned low. He winks at my mom. She whispers, "Thank you," to the security guard and then says, "Donnie, why don't you go watch some TV."

I do what I'm told. I don't want her to regret not leaving me at home.

Once I'm sitting closer to the TV, I can see out of the corner of my eye Mom and the other woman smile at each other. After a moment I see the woman look down at her daughter and then back up at my mom. She whispers, "Cancer."

I swallow hard against my gasp and look at the girl and think, *Please don't die, please don't die, please don't die.* Mom glances at me. I turn my head back to the TV. But out of the corner of my eye I can see Mom give a long look down at Karen. I want to hear Mom say it. I want to hear her say what she pretends I don't know. But she doesn't. Instead she glances at me to make sure I'm not watching, and gives the woman a lying nod that means, *My daughter has cancer too.*

24

It's three weeks later and after midnight when Karen walks into our bathroom and finds me sitting on the edge of the bathtub, holding the new food journal that she hid behind the toilet. That night at the emergency room the doctors told Mom that Karen had messed up her stomach with laxatives. When Karen told me about it later she said she'd taken "a whole shitload of laxatives," and then she laughed and didn't understand why I didn't think it was funny. Mom's taking her to counseling twice a week now. She's still getting small, I can see her body changing. I don't know why I thought she wouldn't get another diary. Maybe because everyone around here pretends like she's better even as she's getting smaller.

"What are you doing?" she asks.

I hold up the notebook. I know she can't scream at me

like she wants to because then Mom will wake up and find out. I'm going to tell Mom anyway. I stand up, still holding the journal, and walk out of the bathroom. Karen follows me down the hall, down the stairs, and out the front door.

The January moon is large. It gives the bare trees shadows. Our socks crunch on the frozen grass as Karen follows me to the small swamp on the side of our house. Heavy frogs poke their eyes out of the slimy water. I walk with numb feet into the swamp, rock to rock, until I am in the center. Karen stays at the muddy edge, her arms crossed in front of her. I squat down and push on a rock, feel that it's loose, and then roll it to its side, leaving a hole that fills with water. I hold the journal up so Karen can see it, and drop it into the hole. Freezing swamp water splashes up at me. I don't flinch. I roll the rock back into place. My voice carries as I walk back to Karen: "There's snakes in here. There's a snake right under that rock. A black one that's as big as my arm. It's wrapped around it already. It's having babies on it, and they're eating the paper and there's nothing left."

I walk by her and don't look back. I let myself think I've taken care of it. Of her. I'll tell Mom tomorrow.

25

If she won't eat, trick her.

It dissolves right away and has no taste. The powder comes in a canister that says PROTEIN POWER! and has a little black plastic scoop to spoon it out with. I don't use the scoop, I have to start much smaller. The first time is when we're both home after school, sitting on the couch, and she has a glass of diet soda on the table. When she goes to the bathroom, I pull the canister out from under the couch, peel off the lid, and pinch a tiny amount between my thumb and finger. I sprinkle it into her soda and stir it with my finger. It dissolves right away. When she comes back and takes a sip, I try not to watch her to see if she notices. She doesn't.

After that I buy two more containers. I keep one under the couch, one in the kitchen in the slow cooker that sits on the counter even though we never use it, and one in my bedroom so I can sprinkle it into her water at night when she gets up to pee.

Dinnertime's a little more complicated. I can't always get alone with her food because she's such a freak about making it just right. It's hardest if she's just eating vegetables or something, because then I have to sprinkle it right on and try to rub it in with my finger. It's best if she makes herself soup or something, because then I can really dump it in. I don't know if it's making a difference. But I have to do something. She's getting so small.

26

"Wait, you mean the French actor with the goiter?" Karen leans over to see what movie ad Mom is pointing at. We have the newspaper spread out in front of our plates on the dinner table, and since last time Karen and I chose, Mom is choosing the movie we're going to see tonight. Karen's having a good week.

Mom opens her mouth in mock offense. "It's not a goiter, it's a mole. And I think he's handsome! Let's go see that. Donnie, you'll like it. It has spies in it."

I poke holes in my carrots and mumble, "Do I have to go?"

"I thought you wanted to go. It has spies in it, maybe someone will get blown up. You'd like that, right?" She winks at me and pats my arm, I lean away from her.

"Donnie, what else are you going to do?" Karen says.

I shrug. I could stay home alone. At least that'd be better than going out with my mom and sister for the third weekend in a row.

Karen rolls her eyes and Mom gives her a quick but cutting glance. "Why? Why don't you want to go?" Karen asks.

I shrug again, and then ask, "Isn't Dad coming home?"

He and I could stay home and they could go out.

Karen waves the potato she has speared on her fork at me. "You know he's not coming home till next weekend. Why do you keep asking that? He said he's coming home next weekend, you know that." She turns to Mom and groans, "Mom, can't you draw him a schedule or something?"

"Shut up," I growl at her. I hate it when she acts like she and Mom are raising me. I hate it when she pretends like she's twenty-seven instead of sixteen.

"Come on, Donnie, don't you want to see the goiter?" Karen holds the forked potato up against her cheek. Mom folds the newspaper and gives me a matter of fact, "Suit yourself. I think you'd like the movie, though. Karen, eat your potato."

Karen takes a tiny bite and then pushes it back against her face. "Come on, Donnie, come to the movies and kiss my goiter."

"Karen!"

I like Mom like this, like she's totally shocked and delighted by something at the same time. "That's just gross." I give Karen my best blank look.

"Come on, Donnie," Karen slurs in a truly horrible French accent. "Come to zee movie and kees my goiter." I don't laugh till she's run around the table and is trying to sit on me, smooshing the potato in my face.

"Kiss my goiter, kiss it! Mom, tell him to kiss my goiter!" She squirms away when I reach for a handful of peas. She knocks them out of my hand and sends them flying. We both freeze, biting down our laughter, waiting to see if Mom will freak out. Mom sighs and takes a sip of water.

"Donnie, kiss your sister's goiter so she can finish eating it." We shriek at that, and Mom giggles into her glass.

I hear Dad's car pull up when Karen and I are on the floor picking up the peas. I give her a "Ha!" before I jump up and run out the front door. I throw my handful of peas into the bushes. I'm starting to regret coming outside to greet him, though. He didn't tell us he was coming. He never does now. He just shows up and acts all hurt if we weren't expecting him. Or he doesn't show up and gets all cranky if one of us asks where he was. His job, he says, keeps him running. On call. You couldn't pay me enough to be on call like that. Never being able to plan on anything.

When he waves to me from the driveway, I can't help but wave back, but I make the movement as small as I can.

"How's things, little man? How's eighth grade?" He gives me a slap on the back and passes me to walk into the house.

"Ninth. It's all right," I say, following.

"Thought maybe you and I could do something this

weekend." He says this from the closet where he's looking for a hanger for his coat. There is none, so he drops the coat on the couch.

"Like what? What'll we do this weekend? Like us, you and me?" I talk to his back as he walks toward the kitchen. He shrugs in response. If I can just get him to pick something, then I've got him. It's harder for him to get out of it if we actually have a plan. Then Mom can say, "You had plans!" and he won't be able to snap, "What, it has to be a holiday every time I'm in my own home?"

Mom and Karen have cleared the dishes—even though none of us were done eating—and are drinking hot tea at the table, looking decidedly, purposefully relaxed. Mom gets up and kisses Dad on the cheek.

"This is a surprise." She motions toward the table. "We're all done eating, but there's sandwich stuff in the fridge if you want. Frozen pizza, too." She sits back down and Dad raises his eyebrows at her.

"You all ate early tonight." He sits down at the table, expectant, and Karen snorts.

"No hello for your old man tonight?" Dad gives Karen what I'm sure he thinks is a charming grin. She won't have it.

"Hello, old man," she answers.

Dad looks from Karen to Mom to where I stand by his side. He sets his jaw and looks back to Mom.

"Sure, I'll have a sandwich."

Mom smiles and nods, and doesn't get up.

I tap him on the shoulder. "Dad, what'll we do this weekend? Could we go hiking or something? Go to the quarry and climb around?"

He doesn't even look at me; his eyes are set on Mom, who hasn't moved from the table. She's sipping her tea. Karen is straight-backed in her chair, watching Dad. Finally Karen says, "Dad, can't you make your own sandwich? Why are you waiting for Mom to make it? I'm sure you make lots of sandwiches at your apartment."

I back away from the table in the moments before Dad answers. I'm practically in the living room when he says, "Karen, I don't think the question is whether or not I can make a sandwich. I think the question is whether or not you'll eat a sandwich."

I get under the front-hall table and peek out from under the edge of the tablecloth so I can see Karen turn pale and look at Mom with wide eyes.

"What?" Her voice is quivering.

Dad has satisfaction in his voice. "Your mom says you're still not eating. She says Marie told her you've stopped talking during your sessions. Mom told me what Donnie found in the bathroom."

Mom reaches over and strokes Karen's arm, all the while glowering at Dad.

"Joseph, can I talk to you for a minute?" Mom stands up and motions with her head toward the living room. Dad doesn't move. He keeps Karen frozen in her seat with his words.

"They're waiting for you up there, Karen. They have your old bed all ready. And this time you are going to listen to what those doctors say."

I whisper, "Asshole, asshole, asshole."

"Joseph!" Mom's got him by the arm and is trying to pull him out of his chair. Karen's come unglued from her chair and is backed up against the counter, gripping the edge behind her.

"Your mom is taking you there this weekend."

Karen gives Mom an openmouthed gaze. Mom shakes her head and says, "Karen."

"I'm not going . . ."—Karen's voice is defiant, shaky—". . . anywhere." I can see her knuckles turning white where she's got the counter.

"Diane? You didn't even tell her?"

Mom shakes her head, still looking at Karen.

"Karen," Dad says, standing up, "get your coat. I'm here, I'll take care of this. I'll take you now."

It is noise and motion after that. Chairs knocked to the ground, teacups tipped over, rolling off the table and shattering. Mom pleading. Dad's weird, low growl. Karen's shrieks. The fight comes into the living room, Karen diving under the table with me, smacking her forehead against my chin. She's got her arms around my chest, she's squeezing me, and I can smell her sweat. I hold on to her. Dad grabs me too when he reaches under, dragging us both out. He's grunting and cursing. Mom's behind him, pressing her shaking hands against her face. Karen's still got me, and I'm saying, "No, no, no, no," trying to hold onto her arms as Dad pulls her away. I can't. I can't hold on tight enough and in a second he's got her in his arms cradled like a baby. He opens the front door with the hand under her legs and tries to step through. I don't think she breaks his nose, but some blood comes out when she cracks it with her knees, jumping out of his arms, and spreading herself in the doorjamb, one hand gripping each side. She's facing Mom and me, her fingers turning white on the doorjamb as Dad tries to pull her outside.

He is a small man. I know this now, after watching him try to pull Karen out of the house. After seeing how when he spreads his hands over hers, trying to pull them away from the doorjamb, their hands are almost the same size. He's not a bear like Amanda's dad at all; he's a little man, like me. He dodges a back kick from Karen, growling "Son of a—"

"LEAVE ME ALONE!" I never knew my sister could sound like that, like the words are being scraped out of her. "DADDY, PLEASE! PLEEEEASE!" She jerks her head from side to side, her hair damp with sweat and sticking to her ruby face.

Mom stands next to me, we've both gone still.

Dad's taken a break, standing behind Karen on the front steps, arms akimbo, panting. He moves to her side, where her flailing legs can't reach him. He leans toward her, laying his right hand on top of hers. Karen's stopped screaming now. He takes his left hand and slowly moves across her shoulders, down her arm, and on top of her left hand, so his body is like an echo of hers. We watch him work his fingers between the doorjamb and Karen's palms, finally pulling her clawed hands away, pulling her back toward him so he can pin her arms to her sides. Karen's head hangs in front of her, she lets her knees buckle, lets her weight fall, so Dad is holding her up. It's all very, very quiet.

Dad leans forward, whispering in Karen's ear.

"Shh. It's all right now. You're all right. We'll get you better. I promise. We'll get you better."

His look at Mom is triumphant. Her look at him is stone.

"Stay here with Donnie."

Karen lets him scoop her up. I'm glad to know that if she were normal, if she were a normal weight, he'd be struggling. It's just her being so small that makes him look strong. He leaves the front door open behind him and keeps purring to Karen as he carries her down the steps. He peels out when he drives away. Mom stays staring at the front door, like she could stay standing there forever. Then she gives her head a shake, like she's rousing herself awake, and says, "I'll call the clinic."

27

Karen might come home early from the hospital. Here's a secret: I hope she doesn't. I'm not ready for her yet. A lot of things happen when she leaves. There's stuff that I try not to notice, like how good it feels to eat a meal without keeping one eye on how many bites Karen takes or wondering how Mom is going to get her to eat something. And it feels good not to eat in front of her. When she's here and we all eat together, every bite is like your teeth don't just cut into the food, they cut into everything that's wrong in this house, and the taste can choke you. Food disgusts her. And when we eat, she watches us like we watch her. She looks fascinated and repulsed at the same time. It's hard to eat a meal like that. And when she's here, there's a lot of stuff we just don't eat: pizza, Chinese food, anything that tastes really good. Just the smell of it will send her flying out of the house yelling an excuse about going to the library or a school play or over to the house of a friend we've never heard of. With her gone, we get really good food delivered almost every night. And the nights we don't order in, Mom gets out her cookbooks, or Dad makes chili or barbecue. Dad is the other thing that happens when she's gone. He's been home almost the whole time. Somehow the long drive to work doesn't bother him anymore. He and Mom still fight, but before it really heats up and I have to go outside, they sigh and then talk about something else.

Here's something else that happens when Karen's gone: Me. I happen. Without her to absorb all the energy, there's some left for me. They don't even really talk about her, at least to me. The most they say is something like "When your sister gets back." Instead they ask me questions about what my day was like and if I can handle how hot the chili is. What's hard is that even though this would be the time for me to tell them everything, I don't. I tell them school is fine. I tell them cool stories that I overhear at school, except I tell them they happened to me. I don't tell the truth because things are too far gone. I can't tell them how things are now because I'd have to explain how they got this way, and the truth is, I have no idea. It's better to play along.

When Karen's gone, she's not the only one recovering. The truth is we need the rest. She leaves and we sleep well. When she's not here, there's no reason to fight about food, there's no one to scream at Mom, there's no one to ask Dad why he even bothers coming home, there's no reason to watch what you say and what you do, because God forbid we piss Karen off and she leaves before dinner. It's not like she leaves and everything gets better. We just take a break and pretend everything's okay. We just need a break.

28

I have an evil nemesis. Two of them. Somehow they've found out my invisibility plan. Every day they wait until I've gone through all of school without anyone saying a word to me. They let me pass through each period unnoticed and untouched. We ride the same bus together. They wait till it's my stop, till I've gotten up and am down the aisle, and then right when I pass them, they say, "Good-bye." And I appear.

Twins. A guy and a girl. "From India, by way of first London, then Virginia," they said on their first day of school, standing up at the front of the class, watching us all look at them. They're unpopular. It was obvious they would be. They wear clothes no one has heard of, and they're polite to the teachers. We watch each other in the halls.

They're going to ruin my life.

29

"Donnie, come in here."

I walk into Karen's room. She sitting cross-legged on her bed, looking at the photo album Amanda made her before she moved. She's been back from the hospital for two weeks, since the beginning of February, and even though none of us says it out loud, she actually looks like she might be getting better. Mom hasn't made her go back to school yet, though. I understand. It might push her off an edge we didn't know was there. A tutor comes every couple of days to go over the work Karen's teachers send. That way, when she's ready to go back, she'll be caught up.

"Sit down."

I sit next to her on the bed. I think, *Ask me how my day was, ask me how my day was, ask me how my day . . .*

"I'm anorexic."

I laugh, and it surprises both of us.

"Why are you laughing?"

I laugh harder. She socks me in my arm.

"It's not funny, Donnie, I have a disease! How is that funny?"

"It's funny," I say, "because you've been anorexic for a fucking year, you've been in the fucking hospital twice, and this is the first time that anybody, you or Mom or Dad or anybody, has said a word about it to me." I'm not laughing any more. I'm fucking furious.

I hear footsteps in the hall.

"Hey, Mom!" I yell. "Karen has anorexia, did you know that?"

The footsteps quicken and Mom stands in the doorway.

"Donnie," she says.

"What? Am I not supposed to know? Did Karen tell little baby brother a big, bad secret?"

"Donnie, you knew Karen was ill."

"Yeah, I knew, but not because you told me. I knew because I pay attention to things. I pay attention to what people say! Guess what else? Dad *left* us! Oh, sure, he stayed here when Karen was in the hospital, but he's not here now, is he? When he comes here, he's a visitor because he moved the fuck out!"

"Donnie."

I get up from the bed and turn to my sister.

"Karen, I'm glad we had this talk. I was actually wondering why we weren't allowed to have butter in the house and why every second of my life has been about making sure your neck bones don't stick out too much. It all makes sense now. Let's do this again sometime." I shove past Mom, go into my room, slam the door, open it, and yell, "This is happening to me too, you know!"

I slam the door again and feel really alive.

30

"Okay. This will be fun." Karen's lying on her stomach in her bed, her arms dangling over the side, holding the coloring book she found in the attic. It's called *The Book About Me!* I sit on the floor, leaning against the bed. She opens the book.

"Okay. Question one. What's your name?"

"Finish your drink first," I say.

Karen picks up the can of weird nutritional liquid she has to drink and gulps down the last of it, and gives an enthusiastic but fake burp. She drops the can in my lap and says, "There. Now what's your name?"

"You know my name."

She flicks my ear.

"This is serious. This is the book about you. I'll fill in the first one about you. Your name is Donnie." She fills in the space in the book with neat, block letters. "Okay, next question. What's your favorite color?"

I shrug. "I dunno."

"What do you mean, you don't know? How can you not know your favorite color?" She looks at me with mock concern. "What are they teaching you in school?"

I shrug again.

"Okay. When you were little, it was green, so we'll put green. Favorite food?"

I stand up. "I have homework."

"Go get it and do it in here. Least favorite food?"

"I don't know."

"Don't be a brat. Sauerkraut. Now, that's a nasty food. How do you spell that? And if you were an animal, what would be?"

I sigh.

"Let me guess. You'd be an endangered North American Wild Idontknow, native to Missouri."

"That's such a Dad joke."

"Dad's not as funny as me. Donnie, why won't you answer this stuff?"

"Because it's stupid."

"Well, yeah, but what else are we going to do?"

I go into my room and get my backpack. When I come back in, Karen says matter-of-factly, "Donnie, I think you need to go on a journey of self-discovery."

"What?" I dump my books out on the floor and give my

math book a light kick before I sit next to it and open it up.

"Seriously. You should drop out of school and hitchhike cross-country"—she sweeps her hand in the air, looks into the distance, and says in a dreamy voice—"discovering what your favorite color is."

"Why?"

"Because it's important!" she snaps, the dreamy voice gone. She's earnest now. "You can't not know these things about yourself, Donnie, because that's just . . . a waste."

She looks hard at me.

I say, "Okay."

"Okay," she says. "Seriously, Donnie."

I laugh, and say loudly, "Okay! What do you want me to do about it now?"

Karen gives me a self-satisfied nod. "A journey of self-discovery. 'Know thyself.' Know who said that?"

"No," I answer.

"Me either. It's not important. What's important is that you know yourself. It's time," she says, taking the math book from my hands, "that you write the Book of Donnie."

31

I really think that someone needs to explain the concept of being a loser to the twins. Because at the rate they're going, saying hello to me every day, it's only going to be so long before some of my loser stink rubs off on them. Don't they have losers in London? Maybe high school in London is the way that grown-ups say the "rest of your life" is here. As in, "Those popular kids are peaking now, and you and the rest of the late bloomers have the rest of your life to shine." Maybe in London everyone shines at the same time. Or maybe it's just like here, where there doesn't seem to be room enough for everyone to be happy at once. I'll be happy. As soon as Karen's better, as soon as Mom and Dad are back together, and as soon as I stop being such a dork. That'll be my time to shine.

For now, though, I'm sticking to the invisibility plan. It's the reason that I can stand here unnoticed, around the corner from where the twins are sitting in front of their open lockers. We're all late to class. Together, but not together. Sheila is crying, "We have names you know? How hard is it to say 'Sheila' and 'Rodney'? Are they so lazy that they can't spare the extra syllables? They can only say 'the twins, the twins, the twins.'"

Rodney starts to answer, but Sheila is on a roll. "And have they never met someone who isn't white before? How could Dad move us to the one school in the whole 'celebrate diversity' United States that had never seen a person of color that wasn't on the telly? Our school in Virginia was *much* more diverse than this one!"

I hear them both stand and close their lockers and begin to walk away. I peek around the corner and watch them, Sheila's angry voice bouncing off the lockers. "I can't tell if they're terrified or repulsed by us! You realize that the one person we've tried to talk to has never even talked back to us? What is wrong with these people? They should be fascinated by us! We're from London, for Christ's sake! There's not a city in this bloody country that comes close to London! Ask us what it's like to live there! Ask us if we miss it! These are not hard questions! But these *are* stupid, stupid people."

I laugh out loud and have to duck back behind the corner as they turn around and look in my direction. Karen's going to love this.

32

"Donnie, come in here."

I stick my head in Karen's room and say, "You're anorexic."

"Very funny. Shut up and come in."

I go in.

"How was school?"

I shrug and flop down on her bed.

"It was fine."

She hits me with her pillow.

"Donnie, I've been home with Mom all day. I'm going out of my mind. You have to tell me how your day was. Tell me a story."

"I told you, it was fine."

"Don't make me hurt you."

Before, when she was well, I would have made her try.

Now, even though I whisper to myself that she's getting better, I am afraid I'll hurt her.

"It was good. The twins waited till I was off the bus and then they yelled at me out the window."

I've told Karen about the twins. I told her a lot of things.

"No shit! Really? What was it today?"

"They said, 'Cheerio pip pip!'"

Karen laughs. "They sound awesome! You should be friends with them."

I shrug. "I've never even talked to them."

"Whatever. You have that whole 'good-bye' game thing. That's good for at least one conversation."

I shrug.

"Donnie, only assholes disappear."

33

Karen's teddy bear lands on my head.

"Donnie, it's seven thirty. Get up. I don't want Mom to come in and yell."

I open my eyes and sit up, curving my back to stretch out the soreness from sleeping on her floor again. I give a big, gasping yawn, and Karen tries to stick her toes in my mouth from where she lies in her bed. I swat her foot away and stand up, tossing the bear on the bed.

"Have fun at school," she says. "And I double dog-dare-you to say hello to the twins before they can say it to you."

She rolls over, snuggles down under the covers, and gives a contented sigh. I drag her blanket off her on my way out of her room.

"Bye," I say, dropping the blanket and closing the door

before her bear can hit me in the head. It gives a soft *thud* against the closed door, followed by Karen's laughing and her stomping across the room to get her blanket.

"Come home right after school, okay?" she calls through the door.

In science class I pull out my notebook. It's still bowed and dog-eared from when I yanked it out from behind my bureau earlier this morning. I have no idea how it got there. I open it up to my notes from yesterday, where I'd written down nine different ways to escape a bear attack. I thought of number ten this morning. It requires freakishly fast reflexes and bull riding experience. I find yesterday's date, February twenty-first, but instead of my How to Beat a Bear list, there's another list altogether. I tear through the notebook.

Every page has a date, and under every date is a too-short list. Not enough to feed a hamster. She hid it in my room. Right under my nose. I am going to kill her.

I slam the notebook shut and stand up, knocking my chair over behind me. Mr. Delancey looks up from his steaming beaker, his eyes bugged out behind the safety goggles.

Everyone else twists around in their chairs. I stand there for a moment. I am not invisible, not at all. Sheila and Rodney stare up at me from where they sit in the row in front of mine.

"Donnie?" Sheila says.

I run out of the room, gripping Karen's food journal in my sweating palm.

34

These are the things you think when you ditch school and tear down the streets of your town, when you run so hard you can't get any air into your shrunken throat and you keep running anyway: The voice in your head is your own, and you are telling your sister to stop. You are telling her you love her and that this is killing her and that she has to please stop stop stop. You are showing her the journal, you are shoving it in her face, you are burning it together. Every step brings you closer till you are at your doorstep, till your key is in the door, till you are shoving it open, till you see her lying in the front hall, till you drop to your knees to revive her.

How did she even get that sweater on? It's a little kid's fisherman's knit sweater, and it's so tight against her chest that I can see what isn't there: Her chest has been deflated, her boobs lie so flat against her that I could be looking at her back and I'd see the same thing. When I scream my sister's name into her face, I can hear my father's voice. I can hear my mother's voice. We are all calling for Karen.

I slap her face. I grab on to the bony rounds of her shoulders and shake. I press my ear against the sweater, trying to hear a thump in her chest. There's nothing. I scream when I can't remember where to press on her chest to make her heart start again. I'm going to press in the wrong place, and I'm going to kill her.

The phone is on the table behind me. I am putting my hands on Karen's chest, and I am kicking backward with my leg, knocking the phone off the table so it lands next to me. With one hand I dial 911, with the other I start to push on Karen. I drop the phone before anyone answers, lay my hands on top of each other, and push down and down and down and down. An ant is chirping inside the phone. I yell in the direction of the phone: "My sister is hurt, this is my address, please come and save her." I yell it three times and then listen. The ant titters. I lean in closer to the phone as I breathe into Karen's mouth, careful not to knock her loose teeth down her throat. The ant in the phone says the ambulance is coming.

35

Dad answers the phone in his work voice, says, "This is Joe, how can I help you?"

I swallow.

"Hello? This is Joe. . . . Hello?"

I can feel the breath build up, pressing out against my lungs, my throat, my mouth. "Donnie?"

I press the phone up against my face. I can hear him swallow, and he whispers, "Did something happen?"

I nod my head.

"Donnie? Did something happen?"

I can hear someone walk into Dad's office, start talking behind him. It's his assistant, Deborah. "Joe. Your neighbor's on the other line . . . ." Her voice breaks up and she gasps. "You should get off the phone."

"Donnie, I'm coming home."

"Come home, Dad."

"I'm coming home."

"Okay."

When he takes the phone away from his ear, I can hear Deborah start to sputter, cry, "I'm so sorry, Joey, I'm so—"

I'd gone into the kitchen to call Dad, so I could still see Mom and she wouldn't hear me from where Elvis had laid her on the couch after wrapping her finger. Now I lean against the kitchen doorway, forcing myself to breathe.

"Mom?"

She doesn't answer, doesn't move. One arm is lying over her chest, the other hangs heavy off the couch, the finger with the puffy white gauze barely touching the carpet. It must be pulling on her shoulder to have her arm hanging like that for so long.

"Mom!" I say it a little louder and I can see the cop who's waiting on the front steps till Dad comes home turn his head and glance inside. Mom still doesn't move. Just her eyes, they keep flicking like she's watching a train pass by. Counting cars. One two three four five six seven.

"Dad's coming home. He's coming home. I think the Durants called him." I wipe at my tears with my sleeve and stare at the back of the cop's head.

I don't know where to go, where to put my body. I think about lying down by Mom on the couch, letting myself go limp. I walk over to the couch, kneel down beside her, and rest my fingers on the couch cushion where she lies. Close enough so I can feel the warmth from her shoulder. Every few seconds I see Karen in front of my eyes, every few seconds I can feel her under my palms. So every few seconds I hold my breath, close my eyes, and wait for it to pass. We stay like that, Mom limp like soft rubber and me still beside her.

She lifts her head when we hear Dad talking to the cop. She lifts it and looks at the door, grips at the couch with nine of her fingers, but doesn't get up. Her face is quaking now, quivering as Dad opens the front door, steps in, and stares for a second at the front-hall floor. The cop must have told him where it happened. Dad turns his head to look at us. We stay trapped there, just like that for a long, long moment. It makes me jump when Mom whispers, "Donnie, your father and I have to go up to our room and talk for a minute." She is looking at me with flat eyes. "Just for a minute. And then I'm going to come downstairs and talk to you. But first your father and I . . ." Dad is helping her to sit up, and then stand. He says, "We'll be down in a minute, Donnie." I watch them walk upstairs and into their bedroom, and then hear them wailing inside. I stay kneeling by the couch, pushing the fibers of the carpet one way, then the other, waiting my turn.

36

You still eat breakfast when someone dies, especially if they die like my sister. I think that's weird. I would have liked everything to stop. But Mom is knocking lightly on my bedroom door, telling me breakfast is on the table and we need to be at the church by ten. Mom's voice is barely there, and she walks like someone is standing on her shoulders.

I'm up already. I'm even in my suit. I found it last night in the attic and slept in it. It smells like my sister because she wore it last, for Halloween two years ago. There's a buzzing sound in my very hot head. It's going to get me through today. If I concentrate on it and look at it with my mind, then my whole body will buzz and I won't feel anything that is happening.

I pass Dad in the hall on the way to breakfast. He grabs my arm and turns me around.

"Donnie?"

He looks like he's searching for something on my face. I search his and see that there are lines cut into his cheeks and around his eyes and mouth. Old-man lines.

"That suit's a little snug on you . . ."

I look down at the suit and realize he's right. I haven't worn this suit in three years. The pants reach my calves and the jacket stops somewhere around my stomach.

"I think you can fit into one of my old suits. You want to come in and try?"

I have a feeling I'm being "handled," the way Dad leads me into Mom's bedroom. I didn't feel crazy when I woke up this morning, but peeling off the suit, I wonder if maybe I'm losing my mind.

The only suit of Dad's left in the closet is the retro one he wore when he married Mom. I put it on and let him tie the tie for me. Dad tells me the tie is red because Mom carried red roses down the aisle.

Breakfast is endless. I feel like every pore of my skin is absorbing what's happening. Every clink of a fork against a plate, every scrape of the chair as Dad gets up for seconds and then thirds. Every tear that falls off of Mom's face and lands in her eggs. I'm sucking it all in, my skin is eating it all. None of us has said a word. It is deafening. I've never had thoughts like this before. I want to tell my parents that I'm not right. I open my mouth and say, "I'm not right."

Dad sips his juice, and Mom scrapes butter against her toast.

"I'm not right!" I say again, louder. Dad looks at me.

"What are you wrong about, honey?" Mom asks in her whisper-voice.

"No, not like that. I'm just not right."

Mom cocks her head to the side, reaches her hand across the table, and puts it on my forehead.

"You're burning up."

I press my forehead against her hand, wondering what it feels like on her palm. She keeps her hand there until Dad comes back with the aspirin.

"Take these. They'll help."

I swallow the pills and immediately regret it. I decide that having a fever is the best way to go through today. I want the filter of the fever to get me through. I want this to be a fever dream. I lie down on the couch and listen to Mom whisper into Dad's neck that she can't do this. It's too much and she can't do it.

The aspirin helps. I fall asleep and dream about hollow-sounding giants that shrink to the size of beans. When I open my eyes, the house is dark and the grandfather clock is chiming that it's four. I've slept through the wake.

"Hey, Donnie."

I know that voice. I roll over and in the darkness see Amanda sitting in Mom's rocker. I guess somebody must have told her. I wouldn't have told her.

"You were sick so I said I'd stay here with you." She's

leaning forward; I can see her hair has grown longer.

"You should leave." I hear myself say it.

She covers her face with her hands and I can hear her cry into her fingers. I don't care. I roll back over so I'm facing the couch cushions.

"I said you should leave." I keep my voice hard, I try to bite her with it.

"Your mom asked me to stay for a couple days." Her voice is just tired, there's no bite to it. I don't let myself feel bad, I just keep my back to her and listen to her walk up the stairs to Karen's room.

37

I wake up long before I realize it. I don't know how long I've been staring at the pattern on the couch cushions. I must have slept down here all night; I'm still in the suit. Somebody put another blanket over me. I am enjoying the blank buzzing in my mind. As soon as I realize I am not thinking about anything, I think about Karen.

I twist around so I can see over the arm of the couch. Mom's at the kitchen table. Amanda is pouring hot water into Mom's teacup and then into her own. I thought maybe I'd dreamed Amanda. She puts the kettle back on the stove and sits in Karen's seat at the table. After a second she slides over into mine.

Mom is patting Amanda's hand and saying, "She really loved to get your letters."

Amanda nods and sips her tea. At the other end of the kitchen Dad leans against the counter and watches Mom in that warning way he has. He hates it when she cries. I think today should be an exception.

"She wouldn't ever let me read them. You know Karen. She'd rather . . . do anything . . . than let me know what was happening in her life. But once in a while she would let something slip, something you were up to. You had a boyfriend?"

Amanda nods and sips. "We broke up," she says. Mom nods. Dad twists his mouth.

"She missed you so . . ." Mom draws a shaky breath; Dad and Amanda hold their breath and watch her. ". . . much." Everybody exhales. It's like watching a rock skip on water, knowing any second it will stop skipping and sink.

"I missed her, too," Amanda says, squeezing Mom's hand. Bullshit. I can't believe she says that with a straight face. She missed my sister so much she stopped writing, stopped calling. Only comes to visit for her funeral, for Christ's sake.

A car horn beeps.

"They must have driven all night," Dad says, and Mom drops her head on the table and cries, "Oh, thank God. Thank God they got here."

"Diane," Dad says. Mom looks up at him, matching his warning with amused astonishment. She sniffs. *"Diane."* Mimicking his voice back to him. It's kind of funny.

"For Christ's sake, Diane." Dad dumps his coffee in the sink, lets the cup fall in with it, and grips the counter. "I'm just trying to hold it together, that's all."

Karen would snort if she saw that. She'd whisper, "Soooo dramatic."

"Well, thank God you're here then. To hold it together for us."

Amanda is pretending to be busy clearing the table.

The horn beeps again, two staccato beeps, and Mom says, "Well, then." She wipes her face on the sleeve of her bathrobe and gets up. Amanda follows her out of the kitchen, and after a second Dad walks out too. They cut through the dining room, I guess not wanting to wake me.

My insides feel heavy and dense, like wet sand packed in a bucket. Even though I kicked off the afghan, it still feels like I'm wrapped in a hot blanket.

I get up and stand behind Mom and Dad and Amanda while Amanda struggles to unlock the front door. I think, *Turn around and notice me, turn around and notice me, turn around and notice me,* but they don't. I wonder if I'm still asleep on the couch. I think *fever, fever, fever.*

It's freezing out. The cold burrows deep into my ears like pins pricking at my brain. The world's gone white bright, and I close my eyes against the glare of the sun off the ice that's covering everything. I gasp against the cold, and Mom, Dad, and Amanda turn around and look at me. They're surprised to see me there. Amanda moves past me, back inside the house. Mom's hand is on my forehead, my face, the back of my neck. Her bandaged finger flutters near my face, wanting to touch it too. She keeps looking at Dad, shaking her head. I concentrate on making my fever fall. It doesn't work.

"We got your prescription refilled," Mom whispers, her eyes looking everywhere but at mine. "Amanda went and picked it up. You can have some toast and then take one. I think it's your ears."

"Do they hurt? Do your ears hurt?" Dad asks, sounding very Dad-like.

I say, "Yeah, they hurt."

He hugs me with both arms.

Amanda comes back out, carrying jackets for all of us. Dad pulls the hood up on mine, the ugly orange one Aunt Janice sent me at Christmas, and cinches it close around my face. We stand at the top of the driveway, watching the movements inside the sedan parked on the street.

"It's Aunt Janice and Uncle Dan," Mom says.

I guess she says it for Amanda, because Dad and I know the chances are very slim that anyone else we know would be driving a pink Cadillac. The engine cuts out; through the glare against the windshield, I can see Aunt Janice looking up at us.

The driver's-side door opens and my uncle pops out, his bushy head of orange hair smooshed down by a hunting cap with earflaps. He looks up at us, waves, and calls, "Hello," and then seems to regret doing it. Then he gives us a really solemn nod and moves around to the passenger-side door to open it for Aunt Janice. I watch the way she reaches her hand out for him, and the way he takes it and gently helps her out of the car. It takes two seconds for Mom to streak by us, skidding down the icy driveway into Janice's arms. I say "Mom" when she runs by. It's like she's leaving us.

Mom grips Aunt Janice's shoulders like the ice under her slippers is trying to suck her down. Aunt Janice says, "Oh, my poor baby, my poor little girl." I don't know if she's talking about Mom or Karen.

Uncle Dan stands for a second next to Aunt Janice and Mom, shifting from foot to foot. Finally he leans over and kisses Mom on the back of her head and walks up the driveway toward us. He looks back toward the car and yells something. Dad mumbles, "Bobby's here?" And from the street we hear Aunt Janice say, "Of course he came," because I guess Mom asked her the same thing.

Bobby hasn't come to our house in two years. Not since he went to college. Aunt Janice says it's hard for him to get back for holidays. Bullshit. He's actually closer to our house now that he's in college than when he lived at home with Aunt Janice and Uncle Dan. I guess if I didn't have to, I wouldn't come to my house either.

Last time Bobby came to visit we sat out on the back steps after dinner. Bobby had this way of asking "How's things?" that made me want to tell him every single thing that was happening in my life. He actually listened for as long as I

wanted to talk. He'd listen and then tell me how all the popular kids end up fat and bitter, still living in their hometown. He
said they'd never go anywhere, never do anything. They reach
their peak in high school, and there's nowhere for them to go
but down. And all the kids that get the crap beat out of them,
he said, well, we're the ones that run the world. It was the same
speech he gave me every time, but it made me feel better.

I remember when Cousin Bobby didn't show up for
Thanksgiving this year. I kept waiting for him to get out of the
car, and he didn't. Even after Aunt Janice told Mom that he
wasn't coming, that his band was on tour, I kept looking out
the window and waiting for him. Things were going really
wrong and I didn't know if I was going to make it. I wanted to
tell him that, that I didn't know if I could make it. I was going
to tell him that I was becoming invisible. I was going to tell
him about Karen.

That night Mom called his cell phone from her bedroom
and whisper-yelled that I was crushed. That I looked up to him
and, damn it, how could he just not show up? I listened from
her bedroom door, wanting to scream at her to shut up.

Aunt Janice and Mom start moving up the driveway, and a
head of wavy, matted hair pops out of the car. Bobby looks
wrecked. He squints up at us and waves his hand. Dad waves
back. I don't.

Bobby ducks back down in the car for a second and
comes back up wearing a worn baseball hat.

"Donnie, I am so sorry. So sorry." My aunt leaning toward me, breathing into my neck, I lean around so I can see Bobby getting out of the car. "Oh! Donnie . . ." She pulls me in between her boobs and holds me there, rocking me back and forth. She's short so she has to pull me down in order to jam my head in there, and now my ass is sticking out and shaking back and forth as she rocks me. I can't breathe because between the hood of my jacket and her boobs, I'm all sealed in.

"Jesus, Ma, let the kid up for air."

She lets go and I pull back, gasping air into my lungs and taking off my hood.

Bobby is standing by the front steps, hugging first Mom and then Dad, all the time looking at me. He reaches out his hand for mine and when I do the same, he yanks me close and puts me in a headlock. I push him off me so hard that he falls on his ass and slides a little on the icy driveway. I can see Mom's mouth shout "Donnie!" and Aunt Janice's mouth just falls open. Amanda looks away. Dad and Uncle Dan are both coming at me. I want to circle Bobby, bounce on my feet like fighters do when they're waiting for the guy they just knocked down to get up so they can knock him down again. But Dad's got me, my arms pinned by my side.

"Ready for me that time, huh, kid?" Bobby's scrambling back up, his palm is scraped a little, and his stupid cap fell off. He's balding on top. Ha. He pulls his cap back on.

"Yeah, I guess," I say. Dad lets go of my arms, and for a second there's this awkwardness with everyone looking at each other and then down at the ground. And then Dad says, "You remember me telling you about Amanda. Karen's best friend. Came all the way from Chicago."

"Yes, of course," Aunt Janice says, and pulls Amanda into a hug. "Diane told me what a help you've been."

I've still got my eyes set on Bobby, who's got his eyes on Amanda. Everybody starts to go up the front steps, and Bobby turns to follow. He stops when he sees I'm not moving, and he looks at me.

"Me and Donnie are going into town to buy some ice cream," he says to Aunt Janice, the last to go in the house. She nods without turning around. Mom pokes her head back out the door. "He's sick, Bobby. Don't stay out too long."

"Man, roll down your window," Bobby says, already rolling his down. The car smells like my aunt, her too-sweet perfume and something sharper and more acrid. The cold air stabs into my ears.

"Where's the ice cream?" Bobby asks, yanking the wheel all the way to the left and U-turning in the middle of our street. I'm not going to tell him where the ice cream is. Let him drive around till he finds it. Maybe he'll get pulled over. Pulled over and arrested for being a prick.

"I'll find it. Sorry, man, I forgot about your ears." He pushes a button on his car door, and my window rolls up. He does his too. I lean back into the seat and let him drive in a direction heading nowhere near ice cream.

"When you were a little kid, you came over to our house, remember that? We went swimming in the pool at the park, and Mom forgot to put those plugs in your ears. You had to go to the doctor and get drops. Remember that?"

I want to not answer him, but the silence is so heavy I give a flat-voiced, "Yeah." Then I remember that day. "Your mom had to sit on me to get the drops in my ear."

"I know!" He's laughing now. "You kicked her in the chin too. That was great."

I remember the feeling of my aunt's face against my heel. How I was so mad at her I wished I'd done it on purpose.

I wish I hadn't said anything just now, I wish I hadn't made him laugh. I wish I'd just sat here silent, making him feel uncomfortable. But now the silence is bothering me, pressing down on me. It's a relief to be mad at him, to feel something that's not about Karen. I don't want him to think we're okay now, though; I don't want him to think we're okay and then ask about Karen.

"Bobby?

"Yeah?" He turns his head so I'm looking him right in the eyes.

"I think you're an asshole."

He turns back to watch the road and looks like he's considering what I said. Finally he nods his head and says, "Okay."

I keep staring at him. He glances at me again. "You have more you want to say to me?"

I shake my head. Bobby nods, pulls the wheel sharply to the right, and pulls the car over.

"Get out of the car." He's already got his door open when he says it, and he slams it shut behind him before I can answer. My heart's racing, and for a second I think he's going to make me walk home. Or maybe he's going to walk home and make me drive the car home. Or maybe he's going to kick my ass and then make me walk home. I watch him walk around the front of the car, and I get that giddy feeling you get when adults lose their shit. When he yanks open my door, I look up at him and try not to laugh. He's obviously making some sort of statement, something he thinks is really, really important for poor freaked-out Donnie. I'm not impressed at all.

"Get out." He's leaning into the car, his face right next to mine. His words are measured, hard. "Don't think that I won't drag you out of there by your tie. Get out of the car."

I get out of the car. But slowly, and as mean as you can be getting out of a car. I hope we fight, I hope he tries to throw me to the ground so I can flip him hard onto his back. I put up my fists. He laughs.

"I don't want to fight you, Donnie."

Yeah, right. He wants to drag me out of the car by my tie so we can make a snow fort by the side of the road. I keep my fists up.

"Why'd you want me to get out of the car, then?"

"Because I want to talk to you," he takes a step forward and I bounce back, raising my fists. He laughs again. I punch him in the chin.

"Dude!" he yells. "That hurt!"

"So, talk! Don't laugh at me!" I yell back. "Talk to me if you want to talk!"

I hate that I don't scare him.

He holds his hands up in surrender. "I'm sorry, I'm sorry. I'm not laughing. I just . . . I would never beat you up!" He laughs again.

"Stop laughing!" I get him in the chin again. This time it's harder and it makes him fall back a step. I raise my fist and he almost trips over himself trying to jump away. It's funny, so I laugh.

"I'll stop laughing if you stop hitting me." He rubs his chin. I laugh again. A big laugh, a laugh that sounds like HA HA HA HA! I laugh and I point at him rubbing his chin.

"Do you feel better?" he asks.

I stop laughing and consider. Yes. Yes, I do feel better. I nod my head and gasp out, "Don't think that I won't drag you out of there by your tie!"

Bobby shrugs. "I wanted you out of the car. It worked, didn't it?" I let him sling his arm over my shoulders. I let him pull me into him. I let him hold me there. I know what this is. This is the point when I laugh till I cry. I miss my sister. If this were a movie, she would throw popcorn at the screen and whisper to me, "How original." Bobby smells like cigarettes and fabric softener. My laughter's just a giggle now, and it's like when you know you're going to throw up and you keep thinking "This is it, I'm about to barf." The first sob's just a sputter out of my mouth. Then the rest comes in spurts, gasps. I hear it inside my head, the sounds of it echoing off my skull. There's nothing except for that sound and the cold against my face. I stop sort of suddenly and try to force more out but just make a low groan, and it sounds false. I think I'm embarrassed, but I'm not sure. Bobby's arm is getting heavy on my shoulders, and I can feel my fever working it's way up again. I sniff, not knowing how to pull away.

"Know what, Donnie?"

I turn to him; he's looking at me.

"I don't know what I'm doing. I don't know what to say to you. There's nothing I can say to you." His dark eyes are pleading with me; I have no idea what to say to him.

I shrug and move away. He opens up my door and I slide into the car. Before he closes it, I say, "It's better if you don't say anything. I won't say anything either. We'll just drive home."

38

When Bobby and I get back to the house, everyone's in the living room looking at the clock, ready to get to the funeral parlor. We don't take off our jackets, because as soon as we walk in, everyone stands up and puts theirs on.

Dad pulls me into the kitchen to give me my medicine and to tell me if I don't feel up to it, I don't have to go. I say, "I want to go," and it makes him cry a little.

In the living room Mom is saying, "Bobby, why don't you take Donnie and Amanda in my car and we'll ride with your mom."

Amanda sits in the back, even though I can tell Bobby wants her to sit up front. I hate them both and wonder if they'd let me ride on the roof rack. I get in the front seat as Bobby's asking Amanda if she lives in Chicago. I turn the radio on before Amanda can answer. Bobby switches it off.

"Right outside."

"I live in Chicago," he says, knocking my hand away from the radio dial.

"Oh, really? I thought you went to college. You drop out?" Amanda keeps looking at me in the side-view mirror. I scowl at her.

"No. I'm taking a semester off. My band's in Chicago. You should come see us."

"Mind if I bury my best friend first?" I like her answer, so I lock eyes with her in the mirror and nod. She nods back.

"Jeesh. Don't come, then. You wouldn't like it anyway."

"Hey," Amanda says, clearly not impressed with Bobby, "were you the one that gave her mom the pot?"

I stare at Bobby. What's she talking about?

"Yeah. It wasn't mine, though," he says.

"Like I care," Amanda says, looking out the window.

"Did it help?" Bobby asks.

"No."

"Oh. I thought her mom . . . I thought she gave it to you . . ."

"What are you talking about?" I ask.

Amanda answers in a flat voice, "Right before I moved, when Karen and I were still . . . your mom got pot from Bobby and gave it to me so Karen and I could get high and she'd get the munchies."

"That's messed up," I say.

"So, what happened?" Bobby asks.

Amanda shakes her head. "So Karen and I went for a walk, I lit up, took a hit, and offered it to her. She looked at me like I'd insulted her. She said, 'I'll get the munchies,' and turned around and went home. I failed my drug test and wasn't allowed on the soccer team at my new school."

"It was good shit, though, right?" Bobby asks with a crooked smile.

Amanda and I both glare at him.

"I have some now if you want . . ." he says, reaching into the pocket of his coat.

"I'm trying to get back on the soccer team, you prick. And we're going to a funeral."

"All right, all right," he says, cringing. "What about you, Donnie?"

Amanda smacks Bobby on the back of his head. "He's on medication, asshole!"

"Jesus," Bobby says.

I climb over the front seat and sit in back with Amanda. She puts her arm around me and pulls me next to her, the way Karen used to. We give Bobby the hairy eyeball the whole way to the funeral parlor.

"Oh, shit," Amanda whispers when we get there. The parking lot is packed and it's flooded with kids from the high school.

"Let us out in front and park the car," Amanda says. Bobby rolls his eyes but pulls over.

The first thing we see is a sign with Karen's name on it that says FUNERAL 11:00 A.M. I'm about to kick it over, but Amanda leads me in the direction the little white stick-on arrow on the sign is pointing. We enter a long room split down the middle by a black-carpeted aisle, with rows and rows of chairs on either side, all filled with people. Mom and Dad are in the front row. There's a casket at the end of the aisle. My sister's in there. I think we both see it at the same time, because as soon as I start to cry, I can hear Amanda crying next to me. She's got my arm entwined in hers and she's got me cinched to her side as we walk down the aisle. All the faces turn to look at us and most cry harder than they already were. They whisper "That's her brother" and "Is that Amanda?" Maddie from the lake is here and we pause next to her seat so she can squeeze our hands and mumble something I can't understand. I'm glad she is here. Bean's and Chris's moms are here too. They don't look me in the eye, they look at Amanda instead. Our principal is here and so is the one from the junior high school, and some teachers too. I could look at these faces all day long. Because if I look at their faces, then I'm not looking at what's in front of us.

"Donnie," Amanda whispers, tugging on my arm. I look in front of me and see that we are standing in front of the casket. Everyone's gone quiet, watching us. They think I'm going to say good-bye to her with all of their eyes on me. I stay standing still. Amanda reaches out the hand that's not squeezing mine and lays it on the casket. She closes her eyes and lowers her head. The fear that I'll regret not touching that smooth wood, that I'm missing some connection to Karen that I'll never have again, sends me lurching forward till both my palms and the right side of my face are resting on the casket. I think, *Come back, come back, come back.* I feel hands on my shoulders and know they are my dad's. He doesn't pull me away. He stands up there with me for a long time, until I feel myself lifting my face, and then a moment later my hands, from the casket.

Here is the funeral: People get up and say we are sad and she was a good girl and a good person and she is at peace now and she is in heaven and we are sad now but should get over it and here is a song that she used to love and she is missed by her family and her friends and listen to this poem read by one of her old classmates and she was so full of life and remember this funny thing she used to do and there's the laughter through tears and I'm sweating in Dad's suit and Amanda's still got my arm and they say Karen is at peace, at peace, at peace.

When it's over, people stand up slowly. I hear some sniffles followed by relieved sighs. Those are the people who got closure from the funeral. Other people are still crying, not getting up from their chairs, sobbing into tissues and being comforted by someone who rubs their back and looks around the room for a way out. Some people turn off their tears like a faucet, grateful the funeral's over so they can stop squeezing water out of their eyes. Other people stand up but still have tears streaming down their faces and don't even try to stop them. That's us: my family, and Amanda. The group hug is accidental. We all reach for someone at the same time. There's some overlap, and we all end up pressed into each other—Dad's shoulder in my ear, Mom's smooth hand on my face, Amanda's hip bone in my stomach. Hands squeeze my suit jacket and pull me in closer. We have tied ourselves. It's right then that I wonder what is going to happen to my family. What are we going to do?

I hear somebody behind us whisper, "They're such a close family." The knot goes slack and we are pulled apart.

There's a line of people waiting to give us hugs on their way into the other room. In the other room are deli platters, coffee, and doughnuts. Snacks. Karen would think that was funny. Here's how it works:

THEM	ME
Stand in front of me looking into my eyes	Try not to look away
Say, "Oh, Donnie."	Nod my head. Yes, that's my name
Pull me into a hug	Tap my palms on their back three times and then pull away
Say, "I am so sorry"	Say, "Thank you"
Look at Mom and say, "Oh, Diane"	Look at Mom and then at the new person standing in front of me saying, "Oh, Donnie"

After nine hugs I sidestep behind Mom and slip out of the room. I squirm away from the hands wanting to pull me close, and walk down the hall. Karen would know how to get out of this. There's a door leading outside that's propped open with an empty can of soda. I walk out.

"Put the can back," Bobby says, hiding whatever it is he's smoking behind his back. I put the soda can back.

It's freezing out. My coat's inside. Bobby takes off his hat and pulls it onto my head and down low over my ears. He eyes me for a second, then takes a drag off the joint and holds the smoke in his mouth for a second.

"Your friend thinks I'm a first-class asshole."

"Yeah."

"You know, I wouldn't have given your mom the stuff if I didn't think it would help. I don't want you to think . . . I really liked your sister. She was a good kid, man."

I nod and wish he would go inside. He holds the joint out to me and says, "First time's free."

I consider it.

"It'll take the edge off. You can float through the day, not even be here. They can't touch you."

"What are you doing?" Amanda says, pushing open the door. "Did you get him high?" she asks Bobby, and then turns to me. "Did he get you high?"

I shake my head.

"What's your problem, man? You're not his mom. Let the kid do it if he wants. Donnie, do you want some?"

They are both looking at me. Do I want to get high? The answer is yes. Yes, I do want to get high. I want to get high enough to float up out of here and far, far away. Apparently I've said this out loud.

"You can't get that high," Amanda says.

"I could get you that high," Bobby says.

"And what happens when he comes down?" Amanda asks.

Bobby shrugs and laughs. "Who says he has to come down? He can just go right back up again."

They both look at me. Apparently I'm supposed to make a choice. Take the joint from Bobby's fingers and pull the smoke deep inside my lungs, while he laughs and says, "Oh shit!" and Amanda goes inside, kicking the soda can and locking us both out. Or call Bobby an asshole and let Amanda lead me back inside to the room of snacks and hugs. I weigh my options, and walk away from both of them.

39

I hurt. All the time. I can't believe how much it actually *hurts*. I look in the mirror and try to make a face that shows how surprised I am at the pain. I think to Karen, *Can you believe how much this hurts?* If she were here, she would ask me what it felt like. I'd have to think about that. Then I'd tell her it feels like a punch in the throat and a hand ripping through your chest and squeezing your heart till it pops. The sort of thing that would happen if I was a spy and I was captured by the enemy and tortured. They'd have to take out what was left of my heart, and I'd survive. The first person ever to survive without a heart. Then I'd quit the spy business and say, "I don't know, boss, my heart's just not in it anymore." Karen would laugh at that and throw something at me.

.   .   .

I can always tell when someone else in the house is with Karen in their mind, remembering something. They get perfectly still, except for their face. Their face makes whatever expressions they are making in their memory. So I'll see Aunt Janice or Uncle Dan or Amanda or Dad or Mom, and they'll look like they've lost a game of freeze tag, standing or sitting completely frozen except they are smiling or frowning or furrowing their brows or mouthing angry words or happy words or looking at her in awe and in love. I do the same thing. When we're in our memories, Karen is very, very alive. It's always a disappointment to come out of it.

I can't stop thinking about the way Karen's neck looked when she left for the hospital the second time. I know how to get the picture out of my head. I'll take a tour of the house. I've done this a bunch of times in the past few days. It passes the time. I imagine that Karen's listening to my silent narration when I do it, that she's learning what life is like here without her.

Let's start upstairs. This is the door to Mom's room. Dad would say it's his door too, but we won't get into that now. The snuffling you hear is Mom. She just finished crying. She'll start again soon. It's how I know she's still alive in there. The other way I know she's still alive is that Janice makes her open the door five times a day and tries to make her eat. Aunt Janice should have been a nurse. She has the voice down pat. "Diane, it's time to eat your dinner. I know you're not asleep.

Sit up. Do you want tea or coffee? I brought you both. No, you have to have one of them." She loses the nurse's voice when she talks to Mom about Karen. I can't listen when they talk about that. Mom's pain is the same as mine but so different I can't listen to it.

This open door goes to my room. Only half the crap on the floor is mine. The other half is Bobby's. That's his sleeping bag wrinkled up in the middle of the floor. Aunt Janice finally made him take a shower because the smell in my room was starting to waft into the hall. "That's what music smells like, Ma!" He smiled when he said it, and she swatted him on the butt.

This closed door is to Karen's room. We all pretend like we don't go in there. Dad's in there now. He talks to Karen all night long. I can hear him through my bedroom wall. I try not to listen, but I can hear him tell her about what she was like when she was a kid, what he was like when he was a kid, and how he's really, really sorry. Everyone else just opens the door, steps in for a second, and then goes out and closes the door behind them. I do that.

Let's go downstairs and into the kitchen. Oh, look, here's Amanda and Aunt Janice in the kitchen, "taking care of things." That means calling the church and telling them to bring the flowers from the service to a nursing home, freezing half the food the neighbors bring over, and telling everyone who calls that Mom isn't talking to anyone but she thanks them for calling. They make a really good team. Amanda told Aunt Janice about how her mom left when she was a kid, and

Aunt Janice made those cooing noises we used to make fun of her for, but Amanda totally eats it up. They're like best friends now. As soon as they see me, one of them puts a plate of food in the microwave for me. I always wander off before it's done. There's lots of time to eat. There's just lots of time in general.

Let's follow the horrible screeching noise that's coming from the basement. There's Bobby, playing what appears to be a ninety-eight-minute-long song on the guitar he carted in his parents' trunk all the way from Illinois. If he's not down here, he's out back getting high or in the den playing Dad's old records and making me and Amanda mix CDs of what he thinks we should listen to. Let's leave before he starts jumping on the old baby furniture and doing scissor kicks in the air. Don't worry, it won't hurt his feelings. He knows I'll come back down soon.

Ready for some air? In the car pulling out of the driveway are Dad and Uncle Dan. Dad must be taking a break from Karen's room. They are always pulling out of the driveway or pulling back in. When they get back from one of their trips, Dad wanders up to Karen's room and Aunt Janice asks Uncle Dan in a low voice where they went. He says they just drive around and stop a lot for hamburgers and ice cream. Aunt Janice rubs Uncle Dan's belly, and he kisses her. He's got a sensitive stomach.

Bobby finds me standing on the front steps. He hands me my jacket and says, "Let's go for a ride." He has good timing. He can always tell when I'm about to jump out of my skin.

We go for rides about as much as I give myself tours of the house. Sometimes Amanda comes, sometimes not. Bobby drives and talks about his band and college and politics. He's smart. The pot hasn't made him dumber, it just takes longer for the smart to come out. He teaches me how to drive in an office parking lot. I'm bad at it, but neither of us cares. There's a lot of squealing tires. We go home to get Amanda to show her what I've learned. She yells at Bobby and then teaches me to drive all over again.

40

Mom says the phone is for me and leaves it on the counter. She watches me pick it up and say, "Hello."

"Hello? Donnie?"

English accents. The twins.

"Yeah. It's me."

"It's Sheila, from . . . from the bus. And Rodney . . ."

"Hi, Donnie."

I can picture them, their heads pressed together, talking into the same phone.

"We wanted to say," Sheila says in her quick-clip voice, "that we're sorry about your sister. We would be . . . We would be so sad if something happened to one of us."

I have no idea what to say to that, so I say, "Oh."

Rodney asks, "When do you come back to school, then?"

I'm glad to know the answer to that one.

"Monday."

"Well, we'll see you Monday, then," he says.

"Yes, Donnie, we'll see you Monday."

41

"Amanda, why did you stop calling my sister?" I've got Karen's tone, the one that makes any question sound like a blunt object hitting you in the face.

Amanda looks up from her coffee. "She told me to."

Bobby tips his chair back so it's propped against the kitchen counter and asks, "She told you to?"

Amanda nods. I can see she's tired. None of us has really slept. The family goes to bed, and the three of us end up in the kitchen, eating the casseroles and cakes the neighbors brought over. I let them play at being my parents. Bobby gives me bad advice about how to deal with the kids at school and Amanda makes me take my medicine. Better than my parents, though, we spend a lot of time behind the house throwing rocks at the shed.

"Bullshit," I say. "You were her best friend. Why would she tell you not to call her?"

"When I came to visit that time, when I left early, we had a fight. I was begging her to get help, and she told me I had to let her go."

I don't believe this.

"Why would she say that?"

"Because it was harder for her to stay sick when she knew how much I cared about her."

"We all still cared about her. Fat lot of good that did."

"I didn't stop caring, Donnie. She wanted me to, but I didn't. I kept calling. Your mom would lie and say Karen was out. Then she would just say, "I'm sorry, Amanda, she doesn't want to talk to you." She and I would make small talk for a while, she'd give me some advice, and we'd hang up. I wrote Karen twenty letters from the time I moved. Your mom has them. By the time I visited, she'd stopped writing me back. I kept writing, even after the visit. Karen would throw the letters out and your mom would pull them out of the trash. Karen blocked my e-mails, they would just end up back in my in-box. I started writing just once every couple of weeks and then once a month, and it became like I was writing to myself, because I knew she wouldn't read them."

"You should have tried harder," I say.

"I thought I was trying harder," she says.

"Not hard enough," I say.

"I know," she answers. She closes her eyes for a long moment.

"You can go to bed," I say. She shakes her head, hard.

"I'm up," she says.

They're both fading, I can see it. They jack themselves up full of coffee and try to stay up with me. They always make it till four A.M. and then come the long pauses in conversation. One of them will doze off, jerk awake, and say, "What'd you say?" and it will be too much of an effort for us to unglue our tongues to say, "Nothing."

I stay quiet and let them both fall asleep in the kitchen chairs. I'm glad they're here. And I'm glad they're asleep. I can think about Karen and not be alone. That's all I really want to do at night, think about Karen. I sit and stare at the darkness through the sliding glass door, and I watch our life flash before my eyes.

The first thing I see when I open my eyes is Amanda looking at me. We both slept with our heads on the table. Bobby's stretched out, snoring, on the floor. I keep my head on the table and swallow back the lump in my throat. They're leaving today. Everyone is. Leaving me with Mom and Dad and the Karen-shaped hole in the universe. Tears are running sideways out of Amanda's eyes and dripping on the table.

"Stay," I whisper. More tears slide down her face.

"Stay," I say again, letting the lump rise up and out.

Amanda reaches out her arm, laying her palm face up, her wrist facing me. I sniff and move my arm so my fingers touch the blue green vein on the inside of her wrist.

"I can't," she says.

• • •

We say our good-byes in the driveway, in the same place we said hello four days ago. Mom and Dad walk Aunt Janice and Uncle Dan down to their car, leaving me at the top of the driveway with Amanda and Bobby.

"Well, kid. Here's my number. Use it. Anytime. Come be a roadie when my band goes on tour." Bobby presses a folded piece of paper into my hand and pulls me into a hug.

Then Amanda and I just stand there nodding at each other and giving sideways looks to Bobby till he says, "Oh. All right. I'll wait in the car." They are giving Amanda a ride back to Chicago.

"You already have my number," Amanda says.

I nod.

"Okay, then," she says, and hugs me. For old time's sake I think, *Kiss her kiss her kiss her kiss her kiss her kissherkissherkissher*. I kiss her. It's amazing. She pulls back and scowls at me, and then laughs and says, "Dude!"

"Ha." I say.

"Your sister would have a cow."

I shrug. "Moo," I say.

"Bye, Donnie," she says. And as she walks down the driveway, she keeps looking back at me and laughing and shaking her head. I know I'll probably never kiss her again. I don't care, because I also know that I'm going to know Amanda forever. And that she's my sister, like Bobby's my brother, and the way to get people to love you is to show them that you love them.

42

I try to calm myself down. They're not here. They weren't in homeroom or first or second period. It's almost lunch now. I don't know what I'm going to do. I shouldn't have even thought about them. I should have come in ready to float through my first day back. I just thought . . . since they called . . .

I've successfully avoided most people by plowing through the halls with my head down. If I knock into someone, they don't get mad, they just whisper in my wake. When I'm at my locker, a few people come up to tell me they're sorry about what happened. They either try to look me in the face or avoid looking at me at all.

Third period ends with the lunch bell, and I decide to go to the nurse and call Mom to come get me. It's my first day back, so they have to give me some slack. I cut through the cafeteria on the way to the nurse's office, head down, ready to knock over anyone in my way. I tell myself it's a shortcut, I don't let myself feel the spark of hope that they will be there.

"Donnie! Over here!"

Sheila and Rodney are sitting by themselves at a round table, both waving wildly at me. Ha. When I walk up to the table, Rodney says, "We had to go to the dentist this morning. We'd forgotten. Sit down."

I sit down.

"I'm Sheila and this Rodney. We've never properly met."

"Hi," I say, and open up my lunch bag. Sheila smiles and nods at me for a long time, then purses her lips and looks at Rodney, trying to tell him something with her eyes. He shrugs his shoulders at her, almost frantically. I see her mouth, *Talk to him!*

I let them off the hook. "So what's it like to live in London? Do you miss it?"

"Yes and yes!" Rodney almost shouts with relief. A few people close by turn their heads. I smile at him. "We were born in India but lived in London with our mum and dad."

"How long have you been here?" This is what it is to have a conversation.

"We've been in the states two years and in this town for one month."

"Two years?" Their accents are so thick I thought they'd just moved here. Rodney leans forward conspiratorially.

"We watch a lot of British telly. Sheila doesn't want us to lose our accents."

"We're not American, so why should we sound like Americans?" Sheila says. "Besides, when Mum has us go live with her, we want to blend. We're going to live with our mum."

Rodney rolls his eyes at Sheila and tells me, "We have dual citizenship. Dad's American. And we're not going to live with Mum in the UK anytime soon." He looks at Sheila. "Where would she put us? Her suitcase?" He quotes someone, I'm guessing his mom, "'The road is no place for a child.'"

Sheila thinks about that for a moment, and then says triumphantly, "Well, for university, then."

She and Rodney are staring at something behind me.

"Donnie," Sheila says in an accent that's thicker than the one she had just a second ago, "there's a strange looking boy standing behind you opening and closing his mouth like a guppy out of water."

I turn around and there's Chris, leaning awkwardly and trying to look unconcerned. He opens his mouth.

"Shut up," I say before he can make a sound, and I turn back around to Sheila and Rodney. I hear Chris walk away.

"Well, then. No more guppy," Sheila says.

After lunch I find a note from Chris and Bean in my locker.

"Sorry about your sister."

I crumple it up and clench it in my fist. I turn to where Chris and Bean watch me from their lockers, and drop the note on the floor.

•   •   •

I eat lunch with Sheila and Rodney every day for two weeks, until it feels almost normal. Almost like a pattern. Almost like friends. I still go to lunch a few minutes late and walk almost straight through the cafeteria, planning every day to walk right on to the nurse's office if I don't see them, or if I do see them and they ignore me. They never do, though. They always smile when they see me. I smile back.

They don't say anything about me walking home from school now. I pretend that it's not strange that I opt to walk home every day. I just don't want them to think that they have to be my friends. If we ride the bus together, there'll be that awkward moment when I stand up to get off and they don't want to invite me over to their house, so they don't.

43

From the far end of the hall, a message comes rolling through the crowd. I keep my eyes on the books in my locker, pretending not to notice that people are saying my name. They are calling it to each other, person to person, till eventually a breathy tenth grader walking by me says, "Phone's for you."

I look up at the crowd of kids walking from the gym toward the lockers. A bunch of them point behind them to the open gym doors and the pay phone on the wall. Next to the phone stands one of those kids that's built like a ruler. He holds the phone up with a long arm and yells, his voice bouncing down the hall, "You want me to take a message?"

I shake my head and try to shout, "No . . . I'll get it," but my voice doesn't carry at all.

The breathy girl rolls her eyes and yells, "He's coming!"

The crowd doesn't exactly part as I push through, but it doesn't push back against me either.

The long-like-a-ruler kid is saying into the phone, "Here he is . . ."

He hands me the phone and walks away. The hall is emptying out, and the bell rings. I'll be late for English. I press the phone to my ear.

"Hello?"

I wait for the voice of Chris or Bean or whoever it is that's calling to tell me my break from being whipping boy is over.

"Donnie?"

Maybe they got Bean's sister to call.

"Yeah. This . . . This is Donnie." I grip the phone, ready to slam it back down on the receiver.

"It's Amanda!"

I drop the receiver. It cracks against the wall before I can pick it up again.

". . . you all right, Donnie?"

"I'm fine. Sorry. Dropped the phone. How'd you get this number?"

"Karen got it last year. We used to call each other when one of us was home sick. How are you?"

I have no idea how to answer the question.

"I'm—"

I'm interrupted by someone yelling "Woo doggie!" into the phone. I have to pull it away from my ear. I press it close again when I hear a familiar voice. "What's up, kid?"

I don't believe this. "Bobby?"

"Yep."

I'm speechless.

"Dude, he's speechless," Bobby says to Amanda. She gets back on the phone.

"He's just passing through, Donnie."

In the background I can hear Bobby yell, "Yeah, that's one way to say it." Amanda laughs.

"We wanted to check up on you. How's school?"

I shrug.

"Do you hate us? I didn't want to tell you about . . . us." I hear her whisper to Bobby, "He's really mad!"

"I'm not mad," I say, which falls only partly in the total-load-of-crap category.

Bobby gets back on the phone.

"School okay?"

I laugh.

"Sorry," he says. "Stupid question."

"That's all right. School's fine. Three more years, right?"

"Drop out now and it's no more years."

I can almost feel whatever it is Amanda has thrown hit him in the head.

"Ow! I take it back, Donnie. Be cool, stay in school. Don't do drugs . . ."

"Donnie." Amanda's back on the phone.

"Amanda," I say.

"You should come visit me." There's a muffled shout behind her, and then she says, "Us. You should come visit us."

"Okay," I say.

"Call me and tell me when you'll come. Dad can talk to your mom, tell her it's all right. Now, go to class."

"All right. Bye."

They shout good-bye multiple times, till I hang up.

Ha! I think. *Phone's for me.*

44

I think back on things that happened. And I think about how if you were to tell stories about us, about our family, you might raise up your eyebrows, and you might say, "Well, no wonder." I bet you think you can pinpoint where it started for her. It's easy to think that, when you can look back at something as a whole. But when you're living it, day by day, it's like you're in the belly of something and you can't see its whole shape from the inside. You don't know that what you're inside of is really a monster. Part of me wants to never tell anything about Karen because people will wonder how none of us really saw what was happening. And because I wonder the same thing.

45

Dad's home. I wonder if eventually he'll be home enough for me to not be surprised when I see his car in the driveway. He switched his shift at work. He leaves way early in the morning now and is home when I get back from school. He misses the traffic this way, and it cuts down his commute time. But he still has the apartment by the plant. I never really thought about how weird it was that Dad had another home that I'd never seen. I guess it'd have to have furniture and dishes and sheets. Stuff I wouldn't recognize.

Mom and Dad are in the kitchen, sitting at the kitchen table. I've interrupted something. They both say "Hello" without looking at me. It's what you call being there for your son.

Mom looks surprised. "What did you say?"

"I didn't say—" I start to say, but realize she's talking to Dad.

"You heard me."

They stare at each other across the table.

"Why would you say that?"

"Because it's true."

Mom looks at her hands and then back over at Dad.

"That's not true. Why are you doing this?"

Dad doesn't answer, he just looks at Mom like he's waiting for her to say something. Mom starts crying.

"I'm not doing this with you," she says. "I don't want to do this." She hides her face in her hands and Dad leans forward over the table.

"Why? Afraid of what you'll say? Say it, Diane. Say what you want to say to me."

"I have nothing to say to you."

"Then I'll say it—"

Mom is up out of her seat, pulling the fabric on Dad's shirt and pleading with him, "Don't—Don't do this."

Dad shrugs her hand away and juts out his chin. "All I said was if you didn't want to have kids, you shouldn't have. You shouldn't have married me, Diane. You shouldn't have had babies with me if you weren't going to take care of them."

Mom's sobbing now, shaking her head. Her knees keep bending a little, like she's going to crumple to the floor, and I can't understand how she's still standing.

"You have nothing to say to that? You killed my daughter, Diane. How is that?"

At first Mom doesn't even scream words, she just

screams, her fists clenched and head down and eyes closed. When she looks up, it is like everything opens—her eyes, her mouth, her whole body is exploding right in front of me.

"Fuck you fuck you fuck you!" She's shaking her finger in his face. "I take care of my babies! Where were *you*? Where have you been? She's getting skinny, she's not eating, something's wrong something's wrong something's wrong! Where were you for me to tell you that? You weren't here! You are never here! You are a monster! And you come and drag my baby out of here like she is a criminal? Why would you do that to her? Why did you think that would help?"

Dad watches Mom scream at him, like he is waiting his turn before he says calmly, "Somebody had to do something, Diane. You weren't doing anything, Diane. You were letting her waste away and hoping that she would get better. You know what they say the causes are. You dieted, you obsessed about your weight, you wouldn't let her eat sweets after school, you made her feel like she had to be perfect." Dad's been reading pamphlets on anorexia.

"Monster," Mom says. "You will rot for what you did to our family. You don't get to be with her when you die, miserable and alone. You will go to hell and you will rot there."

"You—" Dad begins, and Mom opens her mouth, ready to eat whatever he is going to say. They could go on like this forever, living just on their own worst fears.

I use both hands to smash the pan against the stove. I hit it three times, denting the stove right down the middle. On the third swing the pan flies off its handle and crashes into the sliding glass door. Shattering it.

"Look at me! Look at me! Look at me!" I'm screaming. I'm crying. I can't even see. "I am right here. I'm standing right here! LOOK AT ME!"

Dad stands and tries to pull me into his arms. I shove him away.

"You never see me! You only see her, even when she's gone, you only see her. I disappeared so she could get better! I never asked you for anything! I disappeared and you didn't even notice! And now she's gone and *I'm* here! *I'm* here!"

Dad and Mom are watching me, crying.

"My name is Donnie! My favorite color is blue! I like macaroni and cheese and I hate oatmeal and you have to see me now!"

My throat feels like it's bleeding. There's a breeze through the shattered door. I throw the pan handle into the sink and leave them in the kitchen. I say over my shoulder, "Dad. You should go. You don't live here anymore. I want you to be my dad, but you can't do it here."

I ride hard at first, pushing through the resistance of the pedals, wishing it were harder. I ride blindly, seeing what just happened instead of the road in front of me. When I think about what I just said to them, I yell "HA!" and it feels so good I yell some more. It sounds like, "YAYAYAYAYAYAYAAAAAAAAAAAAAAAAAAAAAAAAA!"

I stand up on the pedals and pump harder. The bike rocks from side to side every time I try to slam the pedal through the pavement. It takes a long while for me to calm down, to feel like I've gasped and sweated out every last bit of what happened. When I finally slow down, I can feel the blood still buzzing through my veins, my heart still banging in my chest. I coast and concentrate on breathing slower. I hear what Karen used to say to me when I'd get worked up over Mom and Dad fighting, trying to break through the front door with my five-year-old knees. She'd sit me down on the steps and say, "I'm going to turn you into a snail. A slooow, slimy snail. Watch. Your breath is slowing down. Your heart is slowing down. Your blood is slowing down. You are a slooow, sloooow snail."

I stop pedaling and let the bike slow down, trying to stay upright until it is almost standing still. I totter till I'm finally forced to take my feet from the pedals. I get off and let the bike drop by the side of the road. I sit next to it on the curb, and pull my knees up under my chin. This is what they call staring blankly ahead. It's harder than it looks. I try to keep my eyes unfocused, but they keep honing in on details of the house across the street from where I sit. White shutters upstairs and down. Potted plants shaped like upside-down cones on either side of the front door. I close my eyes. I want to be quiet. I want this to be the quietest the world has ever been. I make myself numb to the hard curb under me, to the rough fabric of my knees under my chin, and to the drying sweat that's chilling on my skin. I numb my nostrils so that the smell of chimney smoke and my own sweat fades to nothing. I imagine skin growing over my ears so that there is no sound of distant traffic or garage doors opening or back doors closing. I know how to disappear. I know that I can close my eyes and curl myself up into my mind where it is dark and I am alone but not alone. My numbed body could unattach itself from the earth and float away and it wouldn't matter. I can just . . . disconnect myself from my body, and my body will disconnect itself from the earth. Did you see the boy floating, arms and legs spread wide, light like a balloon, did you see him floating up till he was a dot in the sky?

It is like someone grabs my shoulders and shakes me once, hard. My eyes snap open and an enormous shiver quakes my body. I jump up, my palms are sweating, and my heart is tripping over its own quick beats. I gulp air and shiver again and fight the urge to dig my hands into the frosted grass and hold on with all my strength before the soles of my feet are facing the sky and I am tethered there like a snagged balloon.

My eyes click from left to right, up to down, trying to find something to focus on, something heavy enough to anchor me. They move so fast it is like watching a slide show stuck on fast forward: the crooked way the bike is lying, a penny caked with mud in the gutter, another front-porch light flicked on in the darkening dusk, a cloud shaped like a cracked walnut. Bike, penny, light, cloud. Bike, penny, light, cloud.

They flick in front of me again and again until I wrench my eyes away and force myself to look straight ahead at the house across the street. I count the white shutters again and again until I feel less like someone with a questionable grasp of gravity and more like a loony counting window shutters by the side of the road. I'm really starting to feel the cold. I want Karen to be here. I want her to take me home. I want her to stand up to Mom and Dad for me.

I count the white shutters again. I look at the mailbox imbedded in a squat stone pillar in front of the house. There's a name printed in careful block letters on the mailbox door. I know that name.

You know how when somebody dies, the people that loved them always say things like, "I know Grandpa Eddie is watching over me" or "I know my mom was smiling down at me" or "I could hear my brother laughing right along with me"? You walk around with this feeling that whoever it is that died is with you all the time. Here's a secret: I don't feel a damn thing. At least not till now. Not until this very moment as I read the name on the mailbox, over and over again.

"Okay," I whisper. "I get it."

The doorbell plays a jingly song I don't recognize. I look behind me to where I dropped the bike at the foot of the front walkway. I could get on it and ride away. Inside the house I hear someone hurrying down the stairs. I wipe my palms on my T-shirt. The front door swings open, and Sheila looks surprised at first and then gives me a wide, toothy smile.

"Hello!" As she opens the door wider, she calls over her shoulder, "Rodney! Donnie's come over!"

I hear Rodney call, "Hey, Donnie!" from somewhere inside the house.

"Well, come in! You must be *freezing*! You're just in time for band practice. We've decided to start a band, and we've decided that you're in it. We'll have hot cocoa first. Well, come on, then!" Sheila reaches out, takes my wrist, and smiles as I let her pull me inside.

This is the Book of Donnie. And this is Chapter One.

Turn the page to read
an excerpt from

Available April 2010

CHAPTER ONE

Who Says Dung Can't Be Fun?
First-years' final duty announced!

(You'll want to hold your noses for this one.)

I'm Gigi Lane and you wish you were me.

Oh my God, that has to be the most powerful affirmation in the history of the world. Dictators don't have affirmations that good.

I tap my fingers on the steering wheel to its undeniable rhythm. *I'm Gigi Lane and you wish were me.* I could rule the world with an affirmation like this. But I think I'll start with Swan's Lake Country Day School for Young Women.

My head nods, my fingers tap, my butt muscles pulse to the music of my affirmation as I cruise the predawn streets of Swan's Lake. I stay on Pleasant Street, aptly named because, according to *The Guide to New England Private Schools*, it "winds its way up and down the wooded hills of Swan's Lake, interrupted only by picturesque hilltop farms."

It's at the top of one of these hills that I pull over to the side of the road for a much needed moment of what my mom, in her bestselling self-help book *Meet Your Tweet: The Girlie Bird's Guide to Finding Her True Heart's Song*, calls an affirmation confirmation.

Turning off the car, I slip off my seat belt and get myself into the official Girlie Bird affirm and confirm meditation pose: legs crossed, arms bent to form the "wings that will carry you home."

I close my eyes, steady my breathing, and listen to my heart. *I'm Gigi Lane and you wish you were me.*

I wake up when my head hits the steering wheel, and frantically look at the clock, relieved to see I was asleep for only two minutes. I yawn and rub the crust out of my eyes. Thank God for natural beauty. Otherwise I'd look a wreck after three nights in a row of just a few hours' sleep.

I yawn again, rest my head against the steering wheel, and gaze out the window over the valley to the wooded hill on the other side. Rising up from the early morning mist, standing proud and tall and sure, is the reason I've spent the last seven months in a hamster wheel.

It is a mansion made of brick and marble and limestone, a gorgeous patchwork of architectural styles, its two turrets standing guard on either side of the steepled roof.

From here, in the dim light of dawn, I can barely make out

the stone steps leading up to the double doors. And above the front doors: a circle of stained glass, twelve feet in diameter, inlaid with the pattern of the Swan's Lake crest. I wait, holding my breath. Beyond the school I can see the sun inching its way above the horizon, and in just moments it is shooting through the stained-glass crest, glinting and sparkling, sending all the colors of those carefully cut pieces of glass spinning out across the valley, and straight into my heart.

I know that there are those who are bitter about their own academic experiences (gym class rejects, etc.), who think that my love for Swan's Lake marks me as a pitiable yet attractive creature who has gotten so caught up in the circus that is high school that I truly don't care about anything else.

I ask you this: What else is there?

And please don't bore me with "There is life *after* high school," that medicating sentiment clung to by girls who cry in the bathroom at school dances. Of course there's life after high school! There is college and all that's beyond. But I'm not in college, am I? No! I'm nearing the end of my third year of high school, and may I be stricken with cystic back acne and a lazy eye if I waste one minute of my high school career pining for the future like some pathetic nerd. If there's one thing I hate about nerds, it's their inability to live in the moment.

The future is *now*! Why is it only the pretty people who realize this?

I glance at the clock again. If I don't pick up my best friend, Deanna, and get us to school by five a.m., there'll be hell to pay.

They hate it when we're late. Fiona says it makes her question her selection decisions, and she *hates* questioning her decisions.

Swan's Lake is like any other high school. We have the usual cliques: the Greenies, the Gizmos, the Deeks, the Bookish Girls, the Glossies, the Cursed Unaffiliated, and so on. And, like any other school, there is a top secret group of senior girls that work with an international network of alumnae to keep the Swan's Lake power structure intact.

Also like at any other high school, the Glossies and the Cheerleaders are top tier: You can't get any more popular. Until senior year, that is.

From your very first day of kindergarten at Swan's Lake, you hear the rumors. A whisper on the jungle gym, a low murmur on the story time rug.

As the years go by, the rumors gain traction. Details. There is a secret club, they say, and everyone knows its name, but only its members are allowed to say it out loud. You relish the danger of whispering it to one another in the last bathroom stall, the one marked OUT OF ORDER. "The Hot Spot," you whisper with gummy-bear breath, pulling the end of your braided ponytail out of your mouth.

By the time you're in eighth grade, your braids abandoned for carefully brushed curtains of hair, your skin nicked and scabbed from newly gained permission to shave your legs, a precious few inches of actual cleavage pushing against your crisp, white triangle bra, by this time you know that every year the Hot Spot has a leader. She is called Head Hottie, and on the day you are taken across the street to tour the Upper School, you see her. She is standing on the landing at the top of the grand staircase that stretches up from the main entrance to the first-floor classrooms. There is a girl on either side of her. Together, the three make up the Hot Spot. They are watching you, all of you, as you file through the front doors, trying not to gasp at the car-size chandelier hanging overhead. The Head Hottie watches as you're led into the front office. She studies each of you and then whispers something to the girl standing on her right. The girl nods and makes a note in the back of an oversize, leather-bound book.

It's called the Hottie Handbook, and there is only one copy, bound in black leather, handed down from Head Hottie to Head Hottie every year since Swan's Lake was founded.

If you're lucky enough to be one of those eighth graders whose name was written down in the back of that book, and if you're further lucky enough not to have your name crossed out later due to an unfortunately horizontal growth spurt or a sudden increase in ugliness, you will be like me. One of the chosen.

A Hottie Hopeful. Who cares that being chosen means spending your junior year proving your worth and your loyalty by performing maddening duties like using Wite-Out on any piece of paper in the recycling bin that has less than three lines of text on it? It's Fiona's right to make us do these things. She's Head Hottie, and Cassandra and Poppy are her second and third in command. We're their Hopefuls. We'll do whatever it is they want us to.

Exhaustion and paper cuts are temporary. The Hot Spot is

forever. Once you're in, you're in for life. Like the mob, but with better fashion and less murder. As soon as you make the jump from Hopeful to Incumbent, you become part of the *Network*. It sounds so . . . classified. And it *is* classified. Fiona won't even tell me how exactly it is the whole *Network* thing works, except to say, "Shut your piehole, Lane! You'll know about the Network when I decide you need to know about the Network."

Want a Swan transferred to a vocational high school with a major in industrial plumbing because you don't like the way she laughs? Done. Freeze the family assets of a Swan who fouls you during gym, causing her tuition check to bounce? No problem. Have a Swan deported, even though she was born in Kansas? Enjoy your "native" Ireland, Katie Pretovka!

Head Hottie is always the most popular girl in school, closely followed by her second and third: in my case my best friend, Deanna, and our hanging participle, Aloha. There is no way someone with substandard social standing could handle, much less deserve, the sort of power we stand to inherit.

I am sure that I am not the only one who is sick and tired of the vulgar media backlash against popularity. Filthy propaganda texts like *Mommy, Why Don't They Like Me? How the Quest for Popularity Is Killing Our Daughters*; snuff films profiling the "evil" popular girl who ends up publicly humiliated at the hands of a vindictive nerd; photographs, collages, folk music, sculpture, dance . . . there is an *endless* list of tools "artists" use to slander, defame, and otherwise vilify popular girls.

And you know what I say to them? *You're welcome.*

Without popular girls like me, artists would have nothing to rail against, nothing to lament in whiny songs, no angst or anger or *feeling*.

At least art is benign. What's harder to handle is the myths.

Myth #1. Popular girls are the reason you're unhappy.

No. *You* are the reason you're unhappy. In my mom's best-selling self-help book *Chicken No More: The Girlie Bird's Guide to Facing the Truth* she says that what holds most people back from success is—get ready—themselves. She says if you can't face the truth about your shortcomings, you will never overcome them. I will give you an example: Daphne "Dog Face" Hall. She's a classic Art Star, one of those girls that wear Converse sneakers and are always crying in the art room. I have done my best to verbally hold the mirror of truth up to Daphne, and she still refuses to truly see herself for the horror show she is.

"Your eyebrows are taking over your face, Daphne."

"I can see your panty line, Daphne."

"You have weird man-hands, Daphne."

"That bra makes your back fat stick out."

"Here's some zit cream."

"And deodorant."

"And mouthwash."

I've given that girl a whole drugstore's worth of product, and she still insists on coming to school looking like a "Before" picture of an ugly-girl magazine makeover.

Myth #2: Popular girls are secretly anorexic cutters cracking under the pressure of having to be perfect.

To this I say, "Ha!" Pressure just makes popular girls get better grades and grow bigger boobs. Anyone who can't handle the pressure doesn't deserve to be popular and will be weeded out by those who do deserve it soon enough.

Myth #3: Popular girls will peak in high school.

They will show up to your ten-year high school reunion and have back fat, a bartending job at Chili's, and a smoker's cough. Aw, the sweet lies whispered at bedtime by parents of sobbing loser children.

Myth #4: Popular girls are just like everyone else. They get pimples, have fat days, and feel misunderstood.

We don't get pimples. And we don't have fat days. Or gas. Also, we look pretty when we cry, we never get athlete's foot or gingivitis, and we always ace pop quizzes.

Myth #5: Popular girls are heartless wenches that delight in the degradation and humiliation of other people.

We are not monsters. We don't kick kittens or trip blind people. If we're mean to you, it's because you deserve it. It's because you've shown a lack of respect, forgotten your place, forgotten *us*. Keeping you down is part of our duty, just like keeping us up is part of yours. The underclass are not expected to have the aesthetic gifts and natural fashion sense that popular people have, so they don't have to strain themselves popping zits or trolling the Internet for sales on fashionable clothing. For all their whining, they are *happy* with the way things are. They have their place, and so do we.

By the time I flash the peace sign to Max, the overnight guard at the entrance of the gated community where Deanna lives, the sun is rising, lighting up what looks to be a perfect early spring day.

I pull into the driveway of Deanna's humongous house and thank God for small favors the ass-ugly Jones Family Minivan is in the garage. Ugly is contagious, even for cars.

The minivan was a gift from one of Deanna's sponsors during her superstar gymnast days. The Jones Family Minivan, as it was officially called, or the JFM to us, got a little rickety after being driven all over the country to get Deanna to her competitions. But Deanna's mom couldn't afford another car when she had to go back to work selling paper products, so the JFM is still limping along.

I give the horn a quick tap. The light in Deanna's room is on, and so is the one in the kitchen. I honk again, louder this time.

"DEANNA 'DEAR HEART' JONES, IF YOU DON'T GET YOUR ASS OUT HERE, I'M GOING TO KICK YOU IN YOUR ONE GOOD KNEE! Good morning, Mrs. Jones!" I call sweetly as Deanna's mom opens the front door and waves to me. I blow her a kiss and then flip down the sun visor so I can check out my bangs in the mirror. I look back to the house, ready to raise holy hell if Deanna doesn't get outside, when I see her giving her mom a kiss good-bye.

Deanna "Dear Heart" Jones.

My best friend, and the girl formerly known as America's New Olympic Hope.

She walks gingerly down the steps and limps across the front lawn toward my car, her feet making trails in the morning dew. She's wearing an adorable but dangerously short cream-colored baby doll dress with gray knee-highs, a pageboy cap perfectly askew over her signature short pixie-cut hair. She looks like a sexed-up version of Tiny Tim. Without the crutch.

"What's wrong, gimp?" I say out the window. "Run out of horse tranquilizers?"

"I showed the neighborhood kiddies how to back-handspring, and my knee went all wonky on me," she chirps, getting into the car. "It'll be good once I'm busy enough to ignore the pain."

I open the glove compartment and pull out a Shake It Cold chemical ice pack, which features a picture of eleven-year-old Deanna in her leotard giving the thumbs-up sign. I shake it up and hand it to her.

"Are you all right to go to school?" I ask, eyeing the swell of her right knee. Seeing the scar still makes my stomach go sour.

She slaps the ice pack on her knee. "Ohmygosh, this is nothing! Once, during a competition, I sprained my ankle so bad it swelled up bigger than my head!" She gives a half-second shudder at the memory and starts dancing in her seat. *"Whaddup, Gigi, let's go to school, got to get educated, don't be a fool!* I brought Pop-Tarts, is Aloha meeting us at school?"

"Yes, you spaz, she's meeting us. God forbid she actually does what Fiona tells her to. She *knows* Fiona wanted us to come to school together for the rest of rush."

"Blah, blah, black sheep," Deanna groans, handing me a strawberry frosted Pop-Tart and taking one for herself. "Be nice, you know you love her."

I hold the breakfast pastry in my hand, feeling its weight. "Do you know how many calories are in this?"

"Zoink!" Deanna plucks the Pop-Tart out of my hand and takes a huge bite out of it. She hands it back. "There, now it's half the calories."

"Thanks?"

"Did I ever tell you how I wasn't allowed to eat enough food to grow boobies?"

I take a bite of the Pop-Tart. It is ridiculously good. "Really?"

"True story." Deanna stuffs the rest of her Pop-Tart in her mouth. "Now I'm trying to eat my way to double-Ds. How am I doing?" she asks, sticking out her still very flat chest.

"Wow," I deadpan, "those are huge."

"You lie and I love you for you it," she squeals, leaning over to kiss me on the cheek, before twirling her bangs into a perfect point hanging between her eyebrows. "Oh! Did you read the *Trumpet* yesterday?"

"I could never find it!" I smack the steering wheel, remembering my frustration. "And I wanted to look after school, but . . ."

I trail off, sighing, and finish my Pop-Tart.

"But you had a special top-secret meeting with Fiona?"

I try for a noncommittal shrug.

"Wait," Deanna says, "you didn't even call me last night. How late were you out with the pretty little fascist?"

"Late," I grumble.

"Why?"

"You know I can't tell you—"

"Can it with the goody-two-shoes bit, sister, and spill. What'd she make you do this time?"

I sigh. "She had me stealing toilet paper from all the rest-stop bathroom stalls between here and New Hampshire."

"She's a freaky deeky!" Deanna howls with laughter. "Did she tell you why?"

I shift in my seat, trying to stretch out the knot between my shoulder blades. "To try and get me arrested? I don't know. She barely said two words to me the whole time."

Deanna reaches over and digs her fingers into my back. "So you just drove around all night, not talking?"

"Oh, she talked. Ow! Not so hard!" I try unsuccessfully to move from Deanna's reach without letting go of the steering wheel. "She just didn't talk to me. She sat in the backseat and whispered on the phone. Ow! I said not so . . . uuugggggghhhh."

The knot releases, I turn into Jell-O.

"That's the spot, right?" Deanna giggles, the fingers of one hand knuckling deep between my shoulder blades. "Could you hear what she was whispering about?"

She pats me on the back, the massage over. I give a happy shudder. "Paint color, I think."

"Score!" Deanna punches the sky. "I bet they're painting the DOS for us!"

"I hope not. She kept talking about the color red, and I'd like to picture the DOS awash in a creamy beige."

"For *real*!" Deanna agrees. "Very relaxing. Speaking of, I heard there's a giant fountain in the DOS with a statue of Ms. Cady as Poseidon in the middle."

"Just how big do you think the DOS is?" I laugh.

Deanna grins. "If it's big enough for a pool, how could it not be big enough for a fountain?"

"You have a point."

"Did Fiona buy you snacks at least?"

I snort. "She made me buy them. I think I got a chemical burn from eating too many Atomic Fire Balls. Where was the *Trumpet*, anyway?"

The Trumpet of the Swan is our school newspaper, run by a clique called the Voice of the People, otherwise known as the Vox Foxes. They dress in pencil skirts, silk blouses, and pumps, with sheer stockings. They tend to move only as a group, and cruising down the hall wearing coordinating matte red lipstick, they look like a formidable army of secretaries from a 1960s typing pool.

"In Ms. Cady's coat closet. The one next to those wooden

telephone booths at the end of the second-floor science wing. It was down in the left toe of her trout-fishing waders."

Every morning the Vox Foxes hide the one and only copy of that day's *Trumpet* somewhere on campus. They stopped printing out the full circulation after the Greenies climbed up the south turret, housing the Vox Foxes offices, and chained themselves to the roof until the Foxes agreed to save the earth by cutting their circulation down to one. Since the *Trumpet* started out as a paper venture, tradition dictates that it stay that way. Publishing online just isn't an option.

Usually, the first-years find the *Trumpet*, running around before homeroom yanking open closet doors and crawling under the sagging armchairs in the library, giddy and brimming with innocent joie de vivre. Once they find it, word spreads, and usually at some point during the day everyone takes a few minutes to read it, standing with their head inside the shade of a floor lamp or holding themselves up as long as possible on Ms. Cady's chin-up bar, the *Trumpet* taped to the ceiling above.

"So what'd the *Trumpet* say?" I ask.

Deanna bounces up and down with laughter. "It announced the final duty for the first-years! Holy guacamole, those poor pooper-scoopers are going to *stink*!"

"Wait, what are you talking about? What's the duty?"

First-year duties are the other tradition at Swan's Lake. It may seem a bit coarse to have first-years do things like find and clean *only* the windows shaped like triangles, or have a contest as to who can find and dust the longest line of uninterrupted chair rails, but it really teaches first-years the ins and outs and ups and downs of Swan's Lake.

"So," I ask again, "what's the duty?"

"It's doodie duty!" Deanna shrieks. First-years always work from basically the same list of duties all year, supervised by the sophomores. But the last duty for first-years is one the sophomores get to think up, and it's traditionally something absolutely ridiculous and seemingly impossible. "They have to fertilize all the flower beds with cow poop! *And* it's BYOP—they have to bring in the stinky stuff themselves!"

She howls with laughter, slapping her good knee. "Oh, and the *Trumpet* also said that the ballot box for Founder's Ball queen is up outside Carlisle's office."

"Why do they even bother with a ballot box? Everyone's going to vote Fiona as queen, and Cassandra and Poppy as her court."

"Tradition, I guess." Deanna shrugs and then turns her shrug into a shimmying dance. "*And that's gonna be us next year! The queen's court, baby!*"

My cell phone rings, and when I see it's my dad, I hand the phone to Deanna.

"Hi, Dr. Bruce!" she chirps, and then, "Oh! And hi, Dr. Lane!" She moves the phone away from her face to whisper, "It's both of them." She listens and says, "I know, it *is* an early wake-up! Student Council, you know. Oh yes, she's right here, but she's driving, so she can't talk." Deanna laughs. "I *know* you approve, Dr. Lane!" She lifts the cold pack off her knee and pokes at the scar with her free hand. "It's fine, hurts a little in the morning."

A minute later she's off the phone, reporting to me what they said. "Okay, so your dad is stuck at the hospital working a double. He'll be home around three and will most likely pass out, but you should wake him up when you're ready for him to cook dinner."

I look at Deanna.

"To which your mom said, 'Oh, honey, you don't have to pretend you two aren't going to order out again. Just try to at least nibble a piece of lettuce along with the pizza.' And then your mom said she misses you guys so, so, so much. She's in Vancouver, it's beautiful, and she thinks you should all go there next winter break for some snowboarding. And she thinks you should bring me. Well, she didn't say that exactly, but it was, you know, inferred. Even if all I do is sit in the lodge, show off my scar, and have cute board dudes buy me cocoa." She thinks for a second. "Let's see, I think that's all they said. Oh"—she bats her eyelashes at me—"they both love you, and are proud of you, and want you to affirm and confirm before you start the day, because you're their little Gigi Bird, and they want you to fly."

I laugh. Deanna is the only person allowed to indulge in some light teasing about the fact that both my parents have bought into my mom's self-help theories big-time. My mom says when you tell someone your power statement, it takes away its power. But Deanna says she doesn't need her gymnastics power anymore, so at this very moment she giggles, presses her index fingers to her temples, and murmurs her old affirmation, "Super gymnastic powers . . . go!"

"You know you need a new power statement," I remind her. "My mom can help you come up with one if you want."

Deanna shrugs. "High school is cake compared to gymnastics. No special powers needed."

"If you say so."

I'm Gigi Lane and you wish you were me.

We crank up the stereo and are on our way.

CHAPTER TWO

Free* Haircuts!**
*If you have shoulder-length or longer hair
**We get to keep the hair.

(Do-Goods, we're looking at you—bald kids need your help!)

"Good morning, Ms. Cady!" we both scream as we pass the stone statue of our school's founder sitting proudly atop a rearing horse that guards the bottom of the school driveway. Two first-years, one dangling precipitously from the horse's towering left hoof, and the other sitting atop Ms. Cady's shoulders, look up at us as we pass, their polishing cloths paused.

We're a few minutes early, so we park and blast the heat.

I'm exhausted but antsy, shifting in my seat so I can see the parking lot entrance. "They should be here by now."

Deanna yawns and stretches, taking the ice pack off her knee, poking her scar, and tossing the ice pack back in the glove compartment before leaning back and closing her eyes. "We could take naps until they get here."

"I hope Aloha doesn't show up," I grumble. "Maybe that way Fiona would boot her out of the Hopefuls."

"Be nice," Deanna says, her eyes still closed. "You know Aloha is the best choice for our third. She's been our friend forever."

I try to bite my tongue, but words come out. "Not forever. You and I have been friends *forever*. Aloha's a transfer student. There is no forever, past or future, in our friendship."

"Gigi Lane." Deanna opens one eye and glares at me. "You're being a total butt-wipe."

I pout. "So?"

"So, we've talked about this. Is Aloha your friend?" Deanna, both eyes open now, pokes me when I don't answer. "Gigi!"

"Yes, she's my friend."

"Why?"

"Come on, Deanna." I groan, now regretting the fact that I walked right into a Deanna "Dear Heart" Jones love lesson.

"Gigi, why is Aloha your friend?"

I rush my oft-recited answer out in a sigh: "Because she's funny and smart and *kind of* pretty, and when we were ten, she helped us carry that dog that got hit by a car all the way to the animal hospital and then cried when it died."

Deanna nods. "Very good. I bet your heart grew two sizes just by saying that."

I snicker. "And because who else are we going to pick for our third? Daphne 'Dog Face' Hall?"

She tries not to, but Deanna giggles. "Or Heidi," she says, breaking into a devilish smile.

"Ick. No." I shudder. Heidi is in our year and is on the path to becoming Head Cheerleader, a position that any Swan with barely above-average looks and moderate intelligence would be thrilled with. But earlier this year, when Deanna, Aloha, and I were tapped as Hottie Hopefuls, and Heidi wasn't, she threw a fit. Flying pom-poms; furious scissors kicks; obscene, nonsensical cheers through her tears. It was hilarious. It was all just further proof she wasn't ready for the popularity pressure cooker that is the Hot Spot. "That would have been a total disaster," I say, a little giddy at the thought.

"*Total* disaster. Ooh, there's Aloha." Deanna points out the window.

I look down the hill and see Aloha's black Jeep screech into the parking lot. It roars up the hill and screeches again as she parks next to us, lurching to a stop, her hair flying in front of her face, her forehead almost hitting the steering wheel. Totally unfazed, she rolls down her window, and I roll down mine.

"Whaddup, tramps?" Aloha doesn't look at us, but at her own reflection in the visor mirror as she pops open a tube of lip gloss and smooths it on. "Are we early or are they late?"

I grimace as I watch her pucker her lips and make a kissy face at her own reflection. "Aloha, where the hell have you been?"

Deanna pokes me and mouths the words, *Remember the dead dog!*

I sigh and start again. "You know Fiona wanted us all here on time."

"Slept in," Aloha purrs, flipping the visor back up. "What?" she says with a smirk. "Afraid Fiona will lay into you for not '*controlling your fellow Hopefuls*'?"

"Just get in the car," I growl.

"Hi, Aloha!" Deanna calls. "Get in, I brought you a Pop-Tart!"

"You're the tart, you tart!" Aloha calls back with a wink. She gets out of the Jeep and then makes a point of standing right by my window, smoothing down her hair and straightening her outfit.

Dear God, her outfit!

"Take it easy, Gigi," Deanna murmurs, leaning over me to roll up my window. "Just don't look at her."

I nod. And keep nodding. I'm still nodding as I say through gritted teeth, "But, Deanna, she totally stole my style."

"Dude," she cautions, "we cannot keep having this discussion. You guys have a similar look. That's all. Neither one of you is a style snatcher."

I glance out the window to where Aloha is picking an invisible piece of lint off of her vintage 1970s high-waisted jeans. "Oh, come on!" I whisper-yell. "She knows I have that exact same pair of jeans! What if I had worn them today? What then?"

"Then you would have popped your trunk and grabbed the spare outfit you keep exactly for that kind of emergency."

I shake my head. "But I shouldn't have to!" I hiss, trying to keep my voice down. "She *knows* as well as you do that 1970s nondisco, nonpolyester, nonhippie, non-bell-bottom fashion is my thing! I was the first one to grow out and feather my hair, and I was the one that started wearing those high-waisted jeans she's trying to cram her fat ass into, and I've been wearing dangly gold pendant necklaces for *years*. Plus, I have blond hair, which *clearly* works better for that sort of hairstyle. Her brown hair looks like feathered doggie doo-doo."

"Are you done?" Deanna groans.

I shrug. "Maybe."

"She'll be sweating in jeans today," Deanna finally offers. "It's chilly now, but it's going to be a high of sixty-two."

I glance out at Aloha, who is retucking her chocolate brown silk shirt into her jeans, a snug argyle sweater-vest with a deep V-neck over it.

"I suppose my dress *is* more suitable to the weather." I grin with a deep breath, smoothing down the fabric of my vintage micromini. "She'll stink up that silk before lunch."

"Exactly!" Deanna agrees.

"She's going to smell like roadkill! Thanks, Deanna." I pat her on her good knee. "I feel loads better."

Aloha gets into the car, flipping her feathered hair as she does. "I cannot wait for this rushing bullshit to be over with."

I whip around to glare at her. "If you hate it so much, you can drop out right now."

Aloha shrugs and takes the Pop-Tart Deanna is holding out. "Nah. You'd miss me too much. Besides, if I dropped out, then I'd have to go be a Glossy or a Cheerleader, and there's no way I'm going to demote myself."

I can't even look at her. "You shouldn't be so flippant," I snap. "You should show some appreciation."

"For what? The honor of picking up Fiona's dry cleaning?"

I'm Gigi Lane and Aloha wishes she were me. "Forget it. You just better hope they don't find out how lacking you are in sister-hood. Ms. Cady would be—"

"Ms. Cady was a tramp." Aloha laughs. "Why would I care what she thought of me?"

"She wasn't a tramp!" I turn around again. "She had lovers! And she chose not to limit herself by getting married and giving up all her rights!"

"She was a spinster hag!" Aloha shouts gleefully, clearly loving the fact that I'm so riled up.

Deanna levels a glare at both of us and orders, "Be nice."

Aloha pats her on the head. "Sorry, Dear Heart. Didn't mean to sully your delicate sensibilities."

"That's okay." Deanna shrugs. "You guys just drive me bonkers with your stupid faces."

We're all still laughing when I see a familiar sleek sedan pull into the driveway. "There they are." I wipe my eyes and wonder how, once again, Deanna has made everything okay.

The Jaguar slows as it passes us, my stomach twitching at the tinted windows, knowing they are looking right at us. "Let's go."

We get out and follow along behind the car as it parks, like we're Secret Service agents following the president's car in a parade. We take our places—Deanna and I on the driver's side,

Aloha on the passenger, all of us standing three steps back, our hands clasped behind us. "Like butlers," Aloha snorted the first time they made us do it, to which Fiona responded by making us address her only in pig latin for the rest of the month. When the engine shuts off, we glance at one another and then reach out at the same time and open the doors.

Fiona Shay sits in the driver's seat. She is putting on lipstick. She doesn't even look at me. "We're not ready yet." Next to her is her second in command, Poppy, and in the backseat sits Cassandra.

We close the car doors in unison and barely have time to step back into position before there are three quick knocks on the driver-side window from inside the car. We all reach out quickly and open the doors again. This time they get out.

Fiona steps so close to me I can smell her perfume, the brand of which I never find, no matter how many bottles I sniff at the mall. The scent is like a mix of gardenias and oligarchy.

"You'll wash the car," Fiona orders quietly, looking directly into my eyes. "And clean out the trunk. And when you're done, you will wait outside the DOS for further instructions."

Aloha pretends to stifle her groan when Fiona mentions the Den of Secrecy, and when Poppy, Cassandra, and Fiona all level their stares in her direction, Aloha just smirks at her shoes.

Fiona looks at me. "Control your Hopefuls, Lane."

I nod, swallowing against the dryness in my throat. "Aloha," I say, turning toward her. "School song. Five times."

Aloha snorts.

Fiona glares at me, raising her eyebrows.

"In Latin," I add, "and backward."

Fiona nods her approval and walks away, followed by Poppy and Cassandra. We stand watching them, their perfect hair, their perfect posture, cutting a perfect silhouette of popularity for us to step into next year.

Aloha stops reciting as soon as the three are in the building, and wrinkles her nose. "This car smells like ass."

"It's got a bad case of the funk," Deanna agrees, kicking a piece of something smooshy off the front tire. "Did she make you drive through the dump on the way back from New Hampshire?"

I shake my head. "We used my car for New Hampshire. I dropped her back here to pick up her car."

"Why'd you go to New Hampshire?" Aloha asks.

"That's classified and you know it," I snap. "Go get the hose."

Aloha stares at me for a long moment.

"The hose, Aloha," I say firmly.

After she stomps off toward the shed, Deanna sighs.

"What?" I ask, already defensive.

"You could have told her," she reasons. "You told me."

I shrug. "She doesn't deserve to know. You saw the way she acted, she was a total embarrassment."

"She's just being herself."

"Exactly," I agree. "An embarrassment."

The car *does* stink, inside and out. We take turns holding our breath and leaning into the trunk, the portable hand vacuum bucking as it sucks up bits of glass, metal, and unidentifiable gunk. We spray the whole trunk down with carpet cleaner and scrub, and then stretch an extension cord from the basement so we can blow-dry it with the emergency hair dryer I keep in my trunk.

By the time we're done, it's almost 7:00 a.m., and we still have to find the Den of Secrecy, the Hot Spot's secret meeting room. There are tons of rumors about what's inside—a tanning booth; a movie theater; a trampoline; hammocks slung between imported palm trees; a 360-degree mirror box so you can check out what other people really see when they look at your ass; a pool; a kitchen loaded with goodies; a bathroom fully stocked with every cream, lotion, and serum you could ever wish for; and a walk-in closet filled by the *Network* every spring and fall with fashions so forward no one outside of Europe has even seen them yet.

The deal is Head Hottie gets the key to the DOS the first day of senior year. Unless the Hopefuls can find it before the end of the Founder's Ball. If we find it first, we get to spend the rest of the year hanging out in the DOS with this year's Hot Spot.

"You scabs ready for another exercise in futility?" Aloha asks once we're on the landing of the narrow back staircase.

"Perk up, pups," Deanna chirps. "I bet this time we find it."

Aloha rolls her eyes. "It's so cute the way you're delusional."

We decide to look on Founder's Path, the long hallway that marks the old path from the main house to the shed where Swans built Ms. Cady's stunt plane. Now it leads from the senior locker wing to the main entrance of school in the original mansion. Dusting the two dozen Ms. Cady portraits that line Founder's Path is one of the first duties first-years get, and I remember staring in awe at the various images as I ran my dust cloth over the lines and curves of the gilded frames.

"Let's check behind the paintings again," I decide once we're there, peeking behind an eight-foot-tall portrait of Ms. Cady standing next to a giraffe. "Knock on the wall, see if it sounds hollow. There might be a hidden door we missed last time."

Aloha snorts. "You really think Fiona hoists herself through a hole in the wall to get to the DOS?"

"Shut your piehole and knock, Aloha," I snap, moving on to peek behind a cubist rendition of Ms. Cady jumping out of a biplane. "Unless you have a better idea."

Aloha leans on the wall in front of me, blocking my way. "Oh, I have *lots* of ideas, Gigi. You have no idea what great ideas I have."

I hear someone walking up behind me and turn to see Daphne "Dog Face" Hall stop dead in her tracks, as if my gaze has frozen her to the spot.

"Gross!" I gasp, looking at her.

She blinks.

Deanna looks up from the portrait she's checking to shoot me a warning look, and starts hurrying toward us. "Hey, Daphne," she says with a smile, "what's up?"

"Um . . . ," Daphne mumbles. "I'm just going to the art room."

I can feel a familiar, prickling heat rush up over my scalp. I make a shooing motion with my hands. "So, go then."

Daphne doesn't move, she just stares at me, *blinking*.

The heat lets loose and washes over me, sinking into my skin, incinerating my insides until my ears whoosh with the sounds of liquid fury.

"Get your fat ass off Founder's Path, you stupid, ugly troll," I hiss. I step closer to her, going in for the kill. "You're using the wrong moisturizer, and you have stubby eyelashes."

"Dude!" Deanna says, smacking me on the arm. "Don't be a dick!"

Daphne backs away and then turns, breaking into a herky-jerky train wreck of a run toward the arts wing.

"She started it," I huff, my body cooling as Daphne runs out of sight.

"She's got a face like a popped zit." Aloha yawns.

"You're both evil tarts," Deanna says, "and you're going straight to hell."

Aloha nudges Deanna with her hip. "Then why are you friends with us?"

Without thinking, Deanna says, "Because if I wasn't around, they'd burn you at the stake for bitchcraft."

"Oh, crap," Aloha groans. Too late, I see Ms. Carlisle, our headmistress and resident fashion don't, walking toward us. There's a reason that in the "Letter from the Headmistress" section of our brochure there's just a picture of the nameplate on her office door.

She's wearing a lavender skirt suit that I am sure is made of polyester. She adjusts her giant vinyl purse, causing the suit jacket to fall open.

"Ew!" Aloha laughs into her hands, covering it with a fake sneeze, as we all try to look away from Ms. Carlisle's too snug skirt. Its waist is directly beneath her chest, and the skirt squeezes its way down her pouchy stomach, over her bulging thighs, to end in a hideous, flouncing petal-cut hem at her knees.

"Good morning, ladies," she crows, smiling so wide her smudged plastic glasses slip down to the tip of her nose. I try not to flinch at the brown stains on her snaggled teeth. I can't believe *that's* the public face of Swan's Lake.

"Good morning, Headmistress," we answer in unison.

"And what are you ladies up to so early this morning?" Ms. Carlisle starts rifling through her ugly purse, digging in up to her elbow.

"Student Council meeting," Deanna says brightly.

"That's nice, dears. You know, Ms. Cady was a big fan of the saying 'The early bird gets the worm.'"

Aloha grumbles, "She probably ate them."

If Ms. Carlisle hears, she doesn't show it. We rush out a quick good-bye as she pulls out her office key, and make our way to the main entrance.

We pass by the main double doors to school, and through the mottled colors of the stained glass we can see the two rows of first-years with morning duties lining up on the front steps.

"Poopers. Foiled again." Deanna sighs. "We're *never* going to find the DOS."

"Nonsense," I snap. "We're not going to be the first Hottie Hopefuls in the history of Swan's Lake to not find the DOS before the Founder's Ball. Now, where are they?"

"Here." We look to where Fiona is walking down the wide, curving main staircase into the entrance hall, her hand running lightly along the dark, polished banister. Cassandra and Poppy follow. "We're here." Cassandra glowers at us as they reach the bottom. "Where were *you?*"

"We finished the car," Deanna offers.

Poppy clucks her tongue. "You were supposed to find us in the DOS."

"Yeah, well, we tried." Aloha smirks. "But we were interrupted."

"You'll have to try harder," Fiona says. "If you don't find it, how in the world do you expect to use it next year?"

"Wait, *what?*" I jump forward. Fiona narrows her eyes at me. I take a step back. "You said we'd get the location on the first day of school next year. That's what you read to us from the Hottie Handbook."

"Yes, that's true," Fiona admits after a moment. "But no Incumbent has ever had to wait to be *given* the location. Usually the Head Hottie Hopeful would have found it by now."

Aloha snorts and I shoot her a quick glare.

"You're too late now anyway," Poppy informs us. "The first-years are here. You'll be supervising them in cleaning the

Oriental rugs from the underclassmen locker hall. We've given the second-years the morning off from supervising. Find us in the DOS before first period."

Aloha snorts again, and Deanna makes a squeaking sound.

Fiona focuses her gaze on me. "I suggest you advise your fellow Incumbents that snorting like a pig or making sweet little baby sounds will not get them out of their responsibilities. If they would rather not be in their current position, they are welcome to clear the cliques and find another home for senior year."

This shuts even Aloha up. Clearing the cliques is this completely humiliating process that transfers go through where they spend a week or so with each clique until they settle somewhere near the bottom. Transfers never get top tier. *Well, most of them don't*, I think, trying not to snarl at Aloha's platform wedge sandals. Fiona and the others walk up the staircase, not looking back at us.

"Do you think the DOS is upstairs, then?" Deanna wonders.

"Could be," I say. "But we've searched up there a dozen times."

Outside the front doors the first-years have started singing our school song, which, following tradition, they will sing louder and louder and more and more obnoxiously until we let them in.

"'We are the sisters of the swan!'" they sing. One of them kicks the door.

Aloha laughs. "Cheeky little brats, aren't they? Should we let them in or make them chew through the doors?"

"'We weave a tapestry of sisterhoooooooood!'" the first-years scream from outside, slapping their palms on the mottled glass inlay.

I nod at Deanna, and she pulls open the doors. Immediately the singing stops, replaced by gasps and squeals of "Dear Heart!" and the mob of girls pushes through the doors, breaking formation in a thundering scuff of ballet flats to surround Deanna.

"Are you leading duties today?" they ask, their legs still too long for their bodies, their chipmunk cheeks just beginning to thin, their bangs finally growing out from the blunt short cuts that mothers of unfortunate junior-high girls insist on. "Can you teach me to do a back kickover?"

They are giggly, and earnest, and young. Until they see first me and then Aloha watching them. They swallow their giggles, try to settle their breath. They change the way they stand, the way they tilt their heads. A hush falls over them. They stare at us, flushed and gulping.

It's like I'm watching the incarnation of my affirmation. I'm Gigi Lane, and every single one of these Swans wishes they were me.

"The rugs in the underclassman locker corridor need to be beaten," I inform them, thrilled at the low, no-nonsense sound of my voice. "There are three rugs. Four of you to a rug. You can bring them out to the garden by the kitchen; there are ropes already strung up for you to hang them. Grab brooms from the kitchen supply cupboard to beat the dust out. Stay away from the Deeks' courtyard; we don't want to have to pay a ransom to get you back. You will return the rugs to position by first bell. Understood?"

They all nod. I stand there, not moving, not speaking for a long moment. Beside me I see Aloha smile at me. I wink at her. "Dismissed."

They scatter like marbles.

Adrienne Maria Vrettos grew up on a mountain in southern California, where she rode dirt bikes and made a mean double-mud pie. *Skin*, her first novel, was published to great acclaim and named an ALA Best Book for Young Adults, an ALA Quick Pick for Reluctant Young Adult Readers, and a New York Public Library Top 100 Books for Reading and Sharing. Adrienne is also the author of *Sight*. She lives with her family in Brooklyn, New York, and can be found at adriennemariavrettos.com.

From the *New York Times* bestselling author

Ellen Hopkins

Crank
"The poems are masterpieces of word, shape,
and pacing . . . stunning." —*SLJ*

Burned
"Troubling but beautifully written." —*Booklist*

Impulse
"A fast, jagged, hypnotic read." —*Kirkus Reviews*

Glass
"Powerful, heart-wrenching,
and all too real." —*Teensreadtoo.com*

Identical
*"Sharp and stunning . . . brilliant."
—*Kirkus Reviews*, starred review

Tricks
"Distinct and unmistakable."—*Kirkus Reviews*

From Margaret K. McElderry Books
Published by Simon & Schuster